The Seventh One

The Seventh One

BY ELIZABETH YATES

ILUSTRATION BY DIANA CHARLES

WALKER AND COMPANY

NEW YORK

Yates, Elizabeth, 1905–
  The seventh one.

  SUMMARY: A man passes through life possessing
in turn seven dogs, each of whom offers him love
in a different way.
  1. Dogs—Legends and stories. [1. Dogs—
Fiction] I. Title.
PZ10.3.Y36Sl   [Fic]   77-18348
ISBN 0-8027-6324-3
ISBN 0-8027-6325-1 lib. bdg.

All the characters and events portrayed
in this story are fictitious.

First published in the United States ofAmerica
in 1978 by the Walker Publishing Company, Inc.

Published simultaneously in Canada by Beaverbooks,
Limited, Pickering, Ontario.

ISBN 0-8027-6324-3

Library of Congress Catalog Card Number 77-18348

Printed in the United States of America

10 9 8 7 6 5 4 3 2 1

Contents

Prologue

Tom was a small boy when he had his first dog, Bre'er; he was more than sixty when he looked into Una's big eyes, took the paw she offered him and clamped to her collar the tag that gave her his name and address. She lifted her head, making a jingling sound with the other tags she wore—license and vaccination. Between Una and Bre'er were five other dogs. Each one had been loved by Tom and had been taught the things a dog should know; each one had loved and taught him in their different ways. He had thought Nell would be the last; now Una had come into his life. She laid her head on his knee and looked at him. He fondled her around her ears. They were on the way to becoming friends.

Bre'er

HE WAS A FAMILY DOG, BELONGING TO THEM ALL
and to the house as much as the furniture did. He was
shaggy and low-slung, with pointed ears and a tail that
never stopped wagging except when it drooped with
some momentary disappointment. If anyone ever
asked Tom or his two older brothers what kind of a dog
Bre'er was, the answer was simple, "Well, he's brown
...", and that generally took care of the question. Bre'er
was part of life to the Wilson family; he always had
been, always would be. He belonged to them all and
was as ready to sit with Mom Wilson in the kitchen
watching her make a pie as he was to keep Pop Wilson
company as he worked in his gardens or as he was to
attend a sandlot baseball game with the boys. Perhaps
he showed a slight preference for this latter, for he was

1

useful in retrieving balls that went over the fence. He could always wriggle under it and find what no one else could easily spot. He had no objection to wearing a red bow on his collar at Christmas, and he made it plain that whatever food the Wilsons ate was more to his liking than what was generally put in his dish. As a member of the family he clearly felt that he was entitled to his share of whatever was theirs.

By the time Tom was ten, Lee and Neal had gone to college, and Bre'er began to attach himself to the youngest member. His bed, used only for appearance, was moved into Tom's room, and he slept on Tom's bed. He took to following Tom to school, preferring to wait in the bushes outside the school door where he knew Tom was than in the bushes outside the house where he knew Tom was not.

"Your dog must be getting pretty old," a friend said one day.

Tom flew to Bre'er's defense. "He isn't as old as me, and I'm twelve."

"Look how grizzled he's getting."

"That's his coat. It shows he's a terrier."

When he went to bed that night, Tom remembered the comment and realized how often of late he had lifted Bre'er up onto his bed instead of calling to him to jump up. Something in him twitched.

By the time Tom went off to college, Bre'er had become a complete homebody. No more sandlot baseball games, no walks to school. "I'll be home at Christmas," Tom whispered as he knelt on the floor beside Bre'er and held the shaggy head between his hands, "to tie the bow on your collar. And this year you're going to have the biggest piece of turkey ever!"

The tail wagged, the ears cocked, but Tom had to admit to himself that there was more grizzle than ever under the chin and around the eyes, and the eyes looked as if they didn't see quite so clearly. Tom stood up quickly; his own eyes weren't seeing too well just then either. At the door he turned back.

"Good-bye, old fellow, take care of Mom and Pop and the house." He closed the door quickly behind him and went out to join his father, who was waiting in the car to take him to the station.

Accounting for himself, Tom said as casually as he could, "I've been telling Bre'er to take care of you and Mom while I'm away."

"He's been doing a pretty good job at that for a long time."

"Yes, a long time." Tom felt safer in admitting it.

"You were two when he came to us, a six-week-old puppy but even then as ready to take hold of life by the teeth as he was any old stick or shoe. He had a lot to do with bringing you up."

"How, Pop?"

"Well, he was always there, for one thing. Neal and Lee were so much older and out playing with their friends most of the time, but we knew you weren't lonely. You had Bre'er, and he developed a kind of responsibility for you. When you started toddling all over the house, exploring, the way a two year old has to do, your mother always felt safe, for she knew you had a faithful follower. More than once she'd hear Bre'er bark and would go to see where he was and what was up. She'd find him tugging at some part of you to keep you from tipping over a lamp or going where he knew you shouldn't be going."

"But he's small, Pop. Even then I must have been twice his size."

"You were, but he had something that made size unimportant. He had a sense of responsibility, and you were his charge."

Tom was silent, trying to recall his first memory of Bre'er and realizing that a lot must have happened before that.

"There was one time that you took it into your head to go adventuring, and you'd got yourself out onto the road. You were walking then. Bre'er couldn't do anything with you, but he knew your mother could, so he went back to the house to find her. When he did, he barked and tugged at her skirt until she went off with him. Between them, they brought you back."

"Funny how much one forgets," Tom said. "Had I gone far?"

"Too far for a two-year-old on his own."

"Did I get scolded?"

"Can't remember, but I do know that Bre'er got the biggest, juiciest bone he'd ever had."

At the bus station they said good-bye as men do, shaking hands. "Take care of Bre'er, won't you, Pop?"

"We'll do that, Tom, you can be sure."

It was just before Thanksgiving that the letter came. Tom took it out of his box with an uneasy feeling. He heard from home every week, but generally the letter was addressed in his mother's handwriting. This time it was in his father's. He took it up to his room to read.

Bre'er just didn't wake up this morning. You'll be home in two days; we'll have the burial then.

Tom felt a surge of anger. He wanted to deny it, the way he had denied an earlier accusation that his dog was showing his age. It wasn't true. This couldn't have happened to Bre'er. He was his friend; he belonged to them all.

When Tom's roommate came in and saw Tom staring out the window, he asked what had happened. Tom pointed to the letter lying on his bed.

"Sorry," Ben said after reading it, "but he was just a dog."

"A dog!" Tom exclaimed. "He was a member of the family."

They had the service as soon as Tom got home, Wednesday afternoon, just the three of them. Tom carried the wooden box from the shed to the corner in the orchard, where Pop had dug a grave in readiness. Tom was surprised at how light the box was.

Pop said, "He used to bury his bones under this apple tree."

"He kept you from climbing too high in it more than once," Mom said.

Remembering made them smile.

Tom shoveled earth over the box and placed a small, flat stone near the trunk of the tree. They stood there silently. There were no words, but there were memories, and somehow each one felt better as they went back to the house.

"He did all that he could do with his life," Mom murmured, "and that's more than you can say for many a human."

"Going on seventeen years is a long time," Pop said, "a long life for a dog."

"I guess I just thought we'd have him forever," Tom tried to explain his feeling.

"You were growing up, and Bre'er was growing old."

It was the first funeral Tom had attended, his first such confrontation in all his nineteen years. The house seemed empty. His bed at night was too big for him, but there was another feeling that he couldn't explain, though he knew it was there. It was as if he and Mom and Pop meant more to each other.

On Sunday night they all went down to the bus station, and Pop gave an answer to the feeling that had been growing in Tom. "The ranks of the living draw closer together, Tom, when someone dear leaves. That's part of the mystery. And the blessing."

Tom was never to forget those words.

Tagalong-too

SHE CAME OUT OF NOWHERE, AND SHE WENT INTO nowhere, but for all of eleven years Tom belonged to her. It was a reluctant relationship at first, then passionate, then possessive, but never sentimental. He was in his senior year at college with three years of law school still ahead when they first met.

Often seen around the campus during the grim days of early winter, she had won for herself the name "the trash-can hound." She was so thin that her ribs gave the shape of her body, so dirty that her color could only be guessed at as somewhere between gray and yellow; her ears drooped, her tail was kept between her legs. She was fearful of a hand outstretched even when it held a doughnut; an arm upraised caused her to take off to a safe distance, then wheel around and stand trembling

8

with lips curled back. Where she went at night no one knew, but during the day she would hang around the back door of the kitchen, doing her best to tip over a garbage can, then running in terror from the clatter made if she succeeded. Tom was not the only one who took pity on her, and he did his best to offer her food, but he was the only one who persisted.

No matter how hungry she looked, he learned that it was no use trying to approach her with enticing food or endearing words, so he took to sitting on the steps of the library with a book in one hand and a pork chop, or something equally appealing saved from his lunch, in the other. At first she drew near but kept her distance, then backed quickly away and disappeared. After a few days she approached Tom and stretched out her nose to sniff at what he was holding, then she fled. It was a week before she took the hamburger he held out to her and made off with it. After another week, with a hand-out every day, she came near enough for him to put his hand on her lightly, just enough to show that an out-stretched hand meant something else besides food.

Tom did not push his luck too far, and his caresses were cautious and brief, but she began to respond to them. One day she let him put his arms around her. With a sigh, she collapsed against him. He held her in his arms, but it was not flesh he was holding, only bones covered with mangy fur. He almost felt sorry for the fleas he saw, thinking what little they must have had to feed upon. He carried her back to his room in the dorm and gave her the first bath she may ever have had. She submitted to it and to the towel he rubbed her with and to the other towel he wrapped her in. Then he cut a class to take her to the vet.

"How old do you think she is?" he asked.

The vet looked at her teeth, at her eyes. "Three years, perhaps, it's hard to tell. Rough years."

The vet shook his head, warning Tom of the problems he might have with a stray of unknown history, but he gave her a rabies shot and one for distemper. He prescribed vitamins and all the food Tom could get into her, as well as a powder to rid her of the remaining fleas. He wished Tom luck but gave no promise of the dog's survival. "If she makes it, bring her back in a month, and I'll spay her for nothing."

"If she makes it," Tom repeated, "I ought to try to find her owner."

"Forget it. She's just one of the all-too-many animals that people dump from a car or abandon because they've become a nuisance. If she loves you enough to tag along with you, I guess you've got yourself a dog."

"Tag!" Tom exclaimed. "She's got herself a name."

She was too easily frightened to be let loose, so Tom kept her with him and always on a leash. She felt safe in his room, but at sight or sound of another person she would retreat under the bed and peer out balefully. She ate best from his hand, and when that same hand brushed her, she soon ceased cringing. The mangy scabs healed, and when her hair began to grow in, a rough yellowish coat appeared. Her eyes brightened and she started to carry her tail up; she even wagged it in sudden brief moments of joy. But she would not go to Ben or anyone else voluntarily, and a hand raised in any kind of gesture sent her scuttling under the nearest piece of furniture. She did not bark, nor had Tom ever heard her whine or whimper. Somewhere along her way she had learned that it was as useless to challenge life as it was to complain about it.

To ease his conscience Tom put an ad in the paper, but no one turned up to claim her. He was glad. It would have been hard to part with her after the months he had worked over her. She had a name that suited her, but as her body filled out and her yellow coat began to shine from good food and constant grooming, Tom decided that she deserved a breed. When people asked him what she was, he referred to her as a Faroe hound, figuring that there were few who had been to the Faroe Islands to know what kind of dogs they raised there. By the time he took her home with him for summer vacation, Tag was a friend of whom he could be proud. ·

She followed him everywhere except when he went down to the cellar, and there she would not go. Some

far distant memory made her wary of a broom, a duster
shaken in the air, or sharp sounds. Tom's parents
moved quietly in her presence and spoke softly, thinking that when she knew there was no intent to harm,
she would be less skittish; but they were to learn, as
Tom had, that it would take more than a few days of
love to offset abuses she had suffered in the past. A leash
in Tom's hand meant safety and often spelled adventure, but let him have a coil of rope over his shoulder
or a length of it in his hands for some task he was about
to do and she would run from him. When pruning trees,
Tom became adept at dragging branches, never raising
them over his shoulder.

Her first showing of affection was secretive and swift,
then she became openly demonstrative. After that she
made it clear to everyone that Tom was hers and,
though she never barked or acted surly in any way, that
she was there to see that no harm came to him.

Much to Tom's father's delight, Tag turned out to be
a hunter such as Bre'er had never been. Her whole
reason for being during that first summer was to rid the
world of woodchucks, the world being for her the Wilson nursery and orchard. Pop Wilson had had a running
battle with them for years in his vegetable garden, but
Tag's first sight of a woodchuck gorging on lettuce was
all she needed. She gave a yelp, ran to the garden,
leaped into the air and landed on the marauder. Shak-

ing it by the neck vigorously, she then tossed the lifeless creature aside, lettuce still crunched between his teeth, and walked away.

"That dog of yours more than earns her keep," a neighbor said when he saw the Wilsons' garden and thought of the ravages in his own. "What kind is she anyway?"

"A Faroe hound."

"What'll you take for her?"

"Not a king's ransom," Tom shook his head.

The vegetable garden was only a small part of the nursery business that had been in the Wilson family for two generations. Tag proved her prowess among the small fruit trees whose bark was the delight of rodents. But even after the acclaim Tag received and relished as a heroic hunter, Tom and his father had to be watchful when pruning trees not to brandish branches in any way that Tag could construe as menacing her.

"Won't she ever forget the treatment she had in the past, Pop?"

"Not if there's anything to remind her of it. Someone sure was mean to that dog."

Tag had come into Tom's life not only with a name but with a motto that seemed to be "Take what comes your way and make the most of it." It was a way of looking at things that was to become meaningful to Tom during the years that followed, years that saw him through college but not into law school. His mother's death after a long illness, followed six months later by his father's, made it necessary for him to take over the family business. There were debts to pay and living stock to be nurtured. Neal and Lee came back for a while with their families, but the best they could give was advice, for their own lives were settled.

"You've got a pretty good partner," Neal commented, looking at Tag sitting close to Tom.

"Sure have. Sometimes I'm thinking of renaming the business and calling it Tom and Tag, Inc., instead of Wilson and Sons."

The years that followed were good years, hardworking years. Tom put aside his plans for law school and devoted himself to raising the best flowers and vegetables, the best fruit trees. He expanded the acreage, hired extra help at planting and harvest, and began to experiment with new strains. Wilson Seeds became well known, and Wilson Nursery Stock was highly prized.

"I couldn't do it without you, old girl," he said often to the yellow dog who was always close to him, "and maybe you couldn't have made it without me."

Tag's tail indicated complete understanding.

One day, while working in the garden, Tom saw Tag become taut, as if responding to some alert. Her ears were cocked, her tail was carried high, every muscle was quivering. Then, without so much as a glance at him, she streaked off across the open field and disappeared into the woods. Her yelp proclaimed the hunt was on. Tom never saw her again.

When she did not return after a few hours, he went in search of her, calling her name in the tone she had always responded to and seemed able to hear even at a distance. His men started to help in the search, crossing the field and going into the woods, checking every burrow and rock pile or wherever earth looked as if it had been pawed or clawed. There was fresh earth near some stones at the base of an oak tree but no signs of any struggle, no yellow hairs or discernible tracks.

At dusk Tom called off the search. "We'll see if she'll come back for her supper; she always has," Tom said, thanking his men. In his heart he had a feeling that Tag would not be back. Wherever the scent or sound had led her, he felt she had gone on her last hunt. She had come into his life from nowhere; it seemed to be in character that she should leave him in the same way.

During the eleven years that they had been partners, Tag conveyed the feeling that she knew what she was doing, and Tom respected her for it. There had been times when he had held her head between his hands, and the look in her eyes made him feel that she knew more of what life was about than he did. He would miss her, but he was not going to question the fact that it was her life and that she had the right to keep it in her own way.

Laird

Tag's legacy was an unmolested garden. It might never be so again; but, for that summer, Tom weeded, fertilized and looked with pride at the way his plants were growing. He could go to bed at night and sleep soundly, knowing that when he returned to the garden in the morning, he would revel at the sight of cabbages growing to near perfection without being half chewed, to broccolis that measured eight to ten inches across the head with families of flowerets ready to come along as soon as the heads were cut. It had been years since he had taken produce to the county fair, but this year he filled out entry slips and went with baskets of his best. A booth was assigned to him, and in it he arranged his entries, as proud of his turnips as he was of his tomatoes, but with a special pride in the cabbages and broccolis. The displays in the other booths made him sure that everything he had brought was of top quality.

He saw no reason to stay with his vegetables, since the judging would not take place until early afternoon, so he went off to see livestock. He admired the cattle, studied the sheep briefly, leaned on the fence by the horseshow ring and talked with friends or strangers. He arrived at the ring where dogs were being shown just at the time the last class, Best in Show, was being judged. The purple ribbon went to a Scottish terrier, a female fully aware of her achievement and making the most of it as she paraded jauntily around the ring with her master for the last time, ears pricked, tail carried high. Everyone near the gate had a word to say to the owner or a pat to give the Scottie as the two started off to the building where the dogs were kenneled. Tom walked beside the owner, for it was in the direction he was going, and conversation flowed easily between them. Every step he took and every word he heard convinced him of the merits of the breed, and of Lady of the Outer Isles in particular, but she was not for sale. Nor would he have wanted her.

However, when he saw a penful of puppies, his heart took a sudden leap, but he shook his head slowly and hardened his heart. They had been sired by a champion, and he knew that their pedigrees put them at a price beyond his reach. He went back to his vegetables, only to see that they were covered with ribbons and that the great cabbage had a purple *GRAND CHAMPION* tied to its stem. That was what did it.

Returning to the dogs, he leaned over the penful of puppies and made his choice: a sturdy little male who looked as if he had all the spirit and pluck that warranted his name, Lord of the Isles.

"I'll call him Laird."

"You've got a champion in two years' time," the owner said, "and you'll more than get your money back once he wins his colors and you put him to stud. He's a wee thing; have you got a basket to carry him in?"

Back to the vegetables Tom went. Within an hour he had sold them all and had pocketed the ribbons and the checks that went with them. He took one of the empty baskets, returned to the Scottish terrier section, and soon was on his way home with a four-month-old puppy on the seat beside him. Small as Laird was, his pedigree read like a map of Scotland peopled with kings and great folk.

" 'Cabbages and kings,' " Tom quoted, looking at the little fellow who was sitting up in his basket and doing his best to be brave but who couldn't help whimpering a bit. Halfway home Tom stopped the truck and picked Laird up in his arms. The puppy snuggled close to him with a sound that could only be interpreted as contentment. "We're friends," Tom whispered, rubbing his hand over the sturdy body.

When Laird was a year old, Tom took him to dog school. The qualities he had shown as a "wee thing" were there and more so. He was brave, loyal, spirited, fiercely independent, and determined to do what he thought was best. He was fun-loving, but aware that life was serious business and that he had work to do. He could be affectionate but in subtle ways, as if too much of a show was beyond him except on certain occasions. He was canny, never eating a bone entirely but hiding some portion of it against a time of need. His deep bark and proud presence were enough to protect the garden against unlawful intruders. And this pleased Tom.

At dog school he learned the commands as much as it suited him to do so. Heel, Sit, Stay, Down, Come—all made sense to him and became part of his vocabulary; anything beyond that he treated as an insult or a waste of time. Tom suspected that some deep memory told Laird he was destined for show rings; he would make himself ready while surrendering none of his independence. Before another summer came around, Tom realized that he had in his care a dog worthy of all the respect he could give him.

When county fair time came, it was Laird, trimmed and combed so that his coat looked its best, who sat on the front seat with Tom, not a basket of produce. At the sight and sound of other dogs, Laird stepped smartly toward them and into the show ring, acting far more ready than Tom for what was ahead. He did well, winning a first handily in a class of the under-two-year-olds of both sexes, and he did equally well with the males under two.

"Give him another year and he'll have a championship," his breeder said, proud of the performance of one of his own. "You're doing the right thing by him."

Life with Laird was like a chess game. He and Tom were forever matching wits, and invariably Laird was the wittier. He had a way of anticipating what Tom wanted him to do and then doing it better or refusing to do it at all. He was forthright almost to the point of embarrassment; his decisions were made instantly, and they were irrevocable. If he liked a friend, a caller, a business associate who came to the house, he would attach himself to the individual, watching every move, following, barking at times to make the person notice the attention he was giving, and wagging his tail constantly. He could as readily turn away disdainfully and leave the room. Sequestering himself in some private place of his own, he would not reappear until the visitor had left the house or driven off in his car.

"I thought you had a dog, Mr. Wilson."

"Yes, I do, but—" Tom had a battery of excuses— "he's just come in from a long walk . . . gone off to sleep

. . . was in a show yesterday." No matter what he said, it never seemed really to explain or satisfy. And there was no use calling Laird, for Tom had learned that when Laird chose to absent himself, he would not appear again no matter how long the visitor stayed.

When the house belonged to him again, Laird would appear quietly and sit in front of Tom. Staring not so much at Tom as through him, his sharp eyes and every inch of his muscular body would say as clearly as words, "Now what did you see in him?"

Tom began to trust Laird's judgments. Looking back over a conversation or a matter of business, he realized there was something about it that had left him uneasy. The people Laird instinctively wanted to avoid were ones that, after a much longer process, Tom decided to avoid too. They were slow in paying their accounts or failed to fill orders promptly or in one way or another proved to be unsatisfactory. Tom was ready to admit to himself after three years of Laird's tutelage that Laird's assessment of character was more accurate than his.

Never was this more evident than the time when Julie MacTeague of Moorland Kennels entered their lives.

For five years now Laird had had *CH.* before his name, and in breeding circles he was well known. He liked nothing better than the show ring and behaved impeccably. Because of this his service as a stud was sought. Female Scotties whose pedigrees were as prestigious as Laird's were brought to Tom by their owners and left for a day, sometimes longer. Laird greeted each one formally but was impatient for the time when he could have her to himself. He knew exactly what was required of him.

Two months or so later, Tom never failed to tell Laird of the puppies he had sired from the mating. "Three males in that litter, Laird, and two females."

As the years went on, Laird more than once was up against one of his progeny in the show ring. The shows were not all at county fairs; there were some at state fairs and those held by breeders; but no dog yet had ever taken a blue from Laird when in the same class.

One afternoon Tom was standing by a show ring, leaning against the fence and enjoying the performances made by different breeds. Laird's class had come off early, and his win had qualified him for Best in Show, but that class did not come until the last. Watching the various breeds, Tom thought how the dogs matched up with their owners. Laird, knowing the day was not over, took the opportunity to rest and curled up comfortably in the grass near Tom's feet and in his shadow. Cockers, Dalmatians, Sealyhams, Saint Bernards—all took their turn; then came the Shelties, females over two years. The breed was one Tom had watched before and taken a liking to.

It was clear from the moment the class was called which one would come out with the blue. Size, conformation, coat, behavior were all there, and something else—absolute attention to her handler as if there was no other person in the world. Tom glanced at his program and read Moorland Dawn—MacTeague. The judge deliberated, and the ten Shelties lined up in the center of the ring waited. One yawned, another took the occasion to have a good scratch, but Moorland Dawn stood in the position she had been brought to, reposed, alert, her head turned slightly up to her mistress. It was clear that communication flowed between them irrespective of the leash.

After his decision was made, the judge directed the winners to make one more circling of the ring. Dawn, with the ribbon held between her teeth, pranced gaily beside her mistress. Looking now at the onlookers leaning against the fence, she acknowledged their applause with a swaying tail.

"Nicely done," Tom said to Julie MacTeague as Dawn came out of the ring.

"Thanks, I can depend on her. She's never let me down."

Laird approached the Sheltie, noses touched, tails moved slowly.

"Behaves beautifully," Tom said.

"And so she should! She got her companion dog certificate when she was two, and she's five now. You've a handsome dog."

"Laird has never let me down either."

"Oh, they know what they're in the ring for, and they love it."

Tom held out his hand. "Tom Wilson, and this is Laird, Champion Lord of the Isles."

She took Tom's hand. "Julie MacTeague, and this is Champion Moorland Dawn."

Tom never knew when it happened, but while he and Julie were talking, Laird left him and settled himself beside Julie, pushing as close as he could to her while Dawn withdrew the length of her leash and put her attention to licking her paws. When Tom realized where Laird was, he dropped the leash, knowing there was no need to hold it.

Conversation came freely for two who had dogs in common, and during it they learned more about their dogs than about themselves.

It was late in the afternoon when the final class of the day was called, Best in Show, and all those who had won best in their separate breeds were in it. Some of the dogs were tired and acted it as they went around and around the familiar ring; some were bored and displayed it; others were so accustomed to the procedure that they behaved like automatons. Dawn stepped along briskly, her eyes glancing up at Julie from time to time. Here was one more thing they could do together; that she liked it rippled from her golden head to the white tip of her tail. The coveted award went easily to Moorland Dawn. In the judge's eyes she had everything —conformation, behavior, response and, as he proclaimed, "sprightly spirit."

Once out of the ring, off their leashes and walking toward the car park, Laird trotted beside Julie Mac-Teague, every now and then giving a sharp bark.

"He's congratulating you two," Tom said. "Nice work, Dawn." He reached down to stroke the lively little lady, then received a quick lick on his hand from her before she jumped up onto the seat beside her mistress. Tom clipped the leash to Laird's collar and soon waved good-bye to Julie.

Back in their own car, Tom and Laird faced each other, and what they had to say was clear. "I'm glad you approve, Laird."

That first meeting was not the last. Tom and Julie met often at shows, then more often without their dogs. As they had discovered in their first conversation, they had much in common, but now they were talking about themselves, their likes and dislikes. Each time they met, they had more to share with each other. Soon even their loneliness away from each other was something they wanted to talk about.

"I can't imagine life without a Sheltie," Julie said.

Tom's reply was, "I can't imagine life without you."

"Yes" was in Julie's smile; concern was in her words. "But the dogs, Tom, what can we do about them?"

Dawn and Laird got on companionably when they met on rare occasions away from shows, but they were two different breeds. Each one had won distinction, which had given them certain responsibilities. Laird had a calendar of appointments set up for him reaching through the year, and his stud fee had become a part of Tom's income. Julie wanted Dawn to have at least two more litters before she was spayed.

"She's a great little mother, Tom, imparting all of her good qualities to her puppies as well as her buoyant spirit."

"The sire also has something to do with that," Tom replied, thinking of Laird's progeny.

"Certainly, and I've always chosen Dawn's very carefully."

"But what does that have to do with us getting married?"

"Oh, Tom!" Julie's tone was as reproachful as it was amused. "Two different sexes, two different breeds, each one with a program, can't possibly live under the same roof."

Behind her words Tom sensed a deeper meaning. Dawn was part of Julie's life; Laird was his business partner.

"We'll have to wait a little while," Julie said softly.

"Yes, but only a little while."

Over the years, Tom and Laird had enjoyed each other's company, but each one had enjoyed the show ring more. What went with it was different for them both, but stimulating; for Tom it meant prizes, stud fees, reports of progeny; for Laird it meant performance and publicity. Tom was like a viewer on Laird's life. Nothing existed between them like the relationship that existed between Dawn and Julie. Tom never spent much time talking with Laird, for he had early learned that Laird always did what he thought he had to do regardless of its effect on Tom.

Late in the summer came the breed match at a neighboring estate. Such affairs were always social and generally in aid of some charity, but many of the top dogs in the country appeared at them. Ranged on the lawn that sunny afternoon were forty or more Scotties, from puppies to experienced performers like Laird. Males and females, they had been groomed to perfection and were ready to show off. Tom, with only one dog, could not enter the class for a brace and intended to sit and watch it, but shortly before it was called, a breeder from out of state approached him. A smart Scotty was beside him and, as often happened, the dogs were introduced first.

"Oriskany Peg."

"Lord of the Isles."

Then the two men gave their own names and shook hands.

"Couldn't bring my dog along; he injured his foot a few days ago and is still limping. Would you let yours team up with mine for the brace? I know yours has proved himself, but Peg did get her first blue today, and it's all in a good cause. You'll handle, of course."

"How about it, Laird?"

No need to ask, he was already in the first stage of acquaintanceship, nose to nose, tail wagging.

Tom gave the dogs a workout in the field. When the class was called, he attached the double lead to their collars and took the brace into the ring. It went off better than Tom or Peg's owner could have believed possible. Peg, smaller, as a bitch should be, and obviously knowing she had something to learn, kept an eye on Laird and did whatever he did. Laird, aware of his importance, acted professionally. When the judge handed Tom two blue ribbons, he nodded and commented, "They're a well-matched pair. How long have they been working together?"

Later, when the dogs were returned to their owners' cars for a deserved rest and the owners went to the house for equally deserved refreshment, Tom was asked if he would consider selling Laird. "I'd like to introduce his blood line into my strain."

Tom smiled. "Would you call it an arranged marriage?"

"Much more, my dear fellow, it was love at first sight. That promises well for their puppies."

"I'll consider it," Tom replied.

"I know what Laird's stud fee is, but what would be an appropriate price for the dog himself?"

Tom half closed his eyes. He couldn't seem to think in terms of dollars, only in terms of Julie.

"What's his age, about seven?"

Tom nodded.

"Just in his prime." Taking out his checkbook, the owner of Oriskany Kennels made out a check to Thomas Wilson. "Will that do it?"

Tom took the check and drew his breath in sharply. It would buy more than a diamond for Julie, but he didn't think she was the kind for diamonds. She'd rather have a new kennel built for Dawn's next two litters. "Thanks," he said.

Later when they went to their cars to let the dogs have a run before the long drive home, Laird had no eyes for or interest in anyone but Peg. They raced each other, rolled on the grass, left smells for each other to investigate, then ran halfway across the field, turned about and came back to stand panting and excited, but it was not Tom that Laird stood beside.

"Good luck, Lord of the Isles," Tom said, ruffling his

dog's head and smiling at him. Laird was not one to whom a final farewell would ever be said, and the wish was scarcely necessary. Laird was one who carried luck with him like a golden coin.

When Tom phoned Julie that night to tell her what he had done, her first words were, "Will you miss him terribly?"

"It was Laird's decision."

There was a moment when only the slight sound of an open telephone line could be heard, then Julie's voice came over it in gentle urgency.

"Tom, Dawn is due to whelp in a little more than two weeks."

"What's that have to do with us?"

"It means we should get married soon, so the puppies can be born in your kitchen."

The sound of a happy sigh came over the line. "Oh, Julie, we've waited so long. It can't be soon enough."

Dawn

THE REIGN OF SHELTIES BEGAN WHEN JULIE MAC-teague became Mrs. Thomas Wilson; it was to last close to twenty years. Initiated by Dawn, it would be carried on by one of her sons, Victor, and brought to its close by a granddaughter, Nell. It had not taken Tom long to understand why Julie had said to him that she could not imagine life without a Sheltie. It was not their charm or their gaiety or their good looks; it was something indefinable that seemed to make a link to a whole other world that was quite apart from that of the human.

"They speak to the heart," Tom said one day.

"They see from the heart," Julie replied.

During that first winter Dawn was occupied with a family of her own, Lad and Lass. They had, of course, been born in the kitchen in a corner that had been prepared for them and curtained off for privacy and against drafts; and Dawn had taken care of them in her own competent way. Julie had known they were due soon, but even palpating Dawn before she bade the dog good-night and went upstairs with Tom had not led Julie to expect them quite so soon.

Coming down to the kitchen the next morning, Julie discovered Dawn behind the curtain. She was lying on one side, relaxed, peaceful, and very proud while two new world adventurers snuggled close to her, almost lost in her fur. They were drawing the milk they needed from Dawn's full teats in the haven of warmth her body made for them. Dawn's eyes and tail spoke for her. She had accomplished a particular work that was hers to do. That she was happy was evident in the way she lifted her head to look up at Julie, then turned it so her tongue could caress the puppies.

"But there's no mess, no . . ." Tom exclaimed.

"I told you she would do everything herself." Julie bent down to stroke Dawn. "Good little mother," she crooned softly.

One puppy then the other tumbled away from the source of milk and rolled into sleep. Julie sat down on the floor and cuddled them in her lap. Dawn got up slowly and stretched herself, then she shook herself and looked at Julie, with a glance at Tom that made her meaning clear.

"Let her out, Tom, please, but she won't stay long, then I'll give her her breakfast. Ours can wait."

Lad and Lass had been spoken for before they were born, and their new owners came to meet them during the first week. Tiny morsels as the puppies were, with eyes tightly closed and ears like flaps buttoned close to their domed heads, their markings were distinctive, and something of their personalities came through even in their present sleeping-eating existence.

They were tricolored. Lad looked as if he might have more white in his ruff than his sister, but with both, the outline of the sable shawl across the shoulders was evident, and each one had the white tip to the tail that was the trademark of the collie clan, whether large breed or small. Lad was to go to a man who had retired from business and taken up cabinetmaking; Lass to a couple who had never had a dog before but in a house now bereft of children wanted liveliness around them, and a dog was the answer, a Sheltie.

Julie had a firm rule that puppies should not leave their mother before they were four months old. Tom wondered if a puppy would not be too much for older people in settled homes and long-ordered lives. But Julie assured him.

"No, no, Tom, Shelties are such bright and sensitive little characters, they soon adapt to whatever situation they find themselves in. They need to feel wanted.

Each one will catch on to what's expected of him, of her. You'll see."

During those first four months Dawn gave the puppies everything they needed. She fed them, washed them diligently, was ready to clean up after them if they didn't quite make it to the newspaper that they early learned was on the floor for a purpose. When she knew that their tiny sharp teeth could begin to serve them, she pushed their noses toward the plates of food that were theirs and refused even their most pitiful entreaties to nuzzle her teats. She could be as firm as she was loving.

At two months, with their eyes wide open and their ears flapping, she began taking them on expeditions outside, introducing them bit by bit to the world. It was as if each one was held to her by an invisible thread. She wanted them to play, explore, discover, but let either one or both go a bit too far and she had them back again, gamboling beside her. Once returned to the kitchen, she would take first one then the other by its scruff, carry it to her corner, and examine it carefully, biting gently at the fur, licking, snuffling, until she was satisfied that there was no twig or grass or bit of earth on their coats that shouldn't be there.

By the time they were old enough to go to their new owners Dawn was quite ready to send them off. She had done all she could, now it was up to them to make their own ways in the world.

Julie always had a few words for the owners about food and the kind of care a Sheltie required. "Just don't be surprised if they're interested in everything that pertains to your life, because what's yours is now theirs. And don't think you'll ever have to speak sharply to them." She gave the low warbling call that she used, and three sets of ears pricked, ready to answer. She raised her hand to indicate they were to stay where they were.

"How about treats?" came a question.

"Yes, indeed, we all need a treat now and then, something special, something out of the ordinary, but the best treat will be your appreciation. They need that."

"Don't we all?"

And so the cabinetmaker and his wife drove off with Lad sitting beside them on the front seat of the truck; and Lass went off on the lap of her new mistress while her new master drove, hard put to keep his eyes on the road for the glances he wanted to have of her. Neither Lad nor Lass looked back. Their separate worlds lay ahead of them.

"Won't Dawn miss them?" Tom asked as he and Julie returned to the house.

Julie had been through this too often not to have a ready response. "She'll have more time for us, Tom. Besides, they'll be back on visits. That will give her a chance to see that everything is going along all right for them."

Dawn came to sit between them, then she lowered herself and crossed her front paws, one over the other. It was the position that always indicated contentment. She looked up toward Julie, then turned her head toward Tom. It was clear that understanding was complete.

A year went by before they heard from Lad's owner, but the letter delighted them:

Can't figure out how that dog knows so much. You'd think he'd been born to the trade. Of course, I've always talked with him a lot, showed him my equipment and what it was for. I soon got to taking him with me whenever I could, and if I couldn't take him, I'd explain to him why and that seemed to put him at ease. He likes to be in the shop with me, and I like having him. If I'm running a saw and don't hear the phone, Lad comes up to me and barks. It didn't take me long to learn that he was doing his best to tell me that somebody wanted me on the telephone.

Sometimes, when carrying a load of trimmings up the stairs, I'll drop one, but if I ask Lad to bring it along for me, he'll deliver it by mouth to wherever I'm working. Funny thing, but I can't ask him to do something for me without saying "please"; then I always say "thank you" when the job is done. My wife takes a rest in the afternoons, but when

Lad knows I'm getting near to quitting time, I tell
him to go get the Missus because she might like to
go for a drive before supper. He'll find her, and if
she's asleep will lick her hand until she wakes up.
We'll be around to see you one of these days. You'll
like to see the way Lad has shaped up. Wonder if
his mother will know him.

Lass's life sounded as if it was all fun and games.

She's a great one for ball playing, fast and quick.
When it's thrown outdoors, she never misses a
catch, and indoors she's good on a bounce. If her
special ball rolls under a piece of furniture when
she's playing by herself, she'll find me and tug at
my skirt until I can come and get it for her so that
she can go on playing her own game again. Outdoors, when some of the neighbor children come
to play with her, she knows when the game's gone
on long enough. She'll run off with the ball and
hide it, stuff it into an old flowerpot or bury it in a
pile of leaves. "That's it for today," she'll say to
them clear as any words; then she'll come back to
the house for a rest. Funny thing, but when she's
ready to play again, she always remembers where
she put her ball and will get it herself.

When Lad and Lass did come for their promised
visits, Dawn's greeting was proprietary. She sniffed
each one thoroughly, then combed their long hair with

her teeth to make sure they were clean right down to their skin. She romped for a while, racing and wrestling as in the old days, then took them off to inspect places they had once all known together. Each one was bigger now than their mother. Dawn tired sooner and made her feelings known to them with a snap of her jaws and a retreat to a private corner. Glad as they had been to come, at a call from their owners the dogs were fully as ready to go, hopping into their waiting cars, settling onto the front seat or a lap to look at the road ahead. When they had gone, Dawn came out of her seclusion to seek Tom or Julie, her tail moving slowly and her whole self saying, "Enough is enough."

"They live in the present," Julie said as she reached down to stroke Dawn and rub her hand over her from head to tail tip in the way she knew Dawn loved, "and yet, when I look deep into a Sheltie's eyes, Dawn's especially, I think they know more about where they've come from and where they're going than we humans do."

Dawn's tail moved slowly as if she was in complete agreement with her mistress's words.

Tom, looking at the two of them, made no comment. He was used to Julie's expressions of feelings about dogs and never questioned them. She had known them in a different way than he had over many years.

"Perhaps," Julie added, "it is because they know

something about the whence and the whither that they can live with such acceptance of the present."

During the years there were letters from owners of one or another of the earlier litters and often visits as well. Dawn always knew her children, and they never failed to treat her with the respect due a parent.

Dawn was nine when she had her last litter. It was a big family, a litter of six, and as with the others, they were already spoken for. She was too well known for her offspring not to be in demand, more as companions than as show dogs, but there were some who won their colors. Julie felt that the show ring was a good place for a dog to prove its points, that obedience trials to prove ability were better, but that home life with people who needed what a Sheltie had to give was best of all.

"We'll keep one," Julie announced as she and Tom surveyed the little family tumbling around Dawn's teats and sucking eagerly when they found what they wanted.

"For us," Tom said.

As they gazed at the six snuggling close to their mother, one of the little males pushed himself away from the milk supply and crawled up under his mother's chin. His tiny tongue reached out and gave her a quick lick, as if love meant as much as milk, then he crawled back to join his siblings.

"That little fellow," Tom exclaimed. "There's something extra special about him."

"Yes, he's the victor," Julie agreed, and Victor he became.

At four months, Wendy, Jeanie, Kiltie, Robin, and Duncan all went off to their new homes, but Victor remained: a companion to Dawn and a delight to Julie and Tom.

There was a daintiness about Dawn that marked everything she did, and there was courage that never quailed. She had always been able to face up to a challenge, and with Victor beside her she was invincible. She knew that a woodchuck had no place in Tom's gardens, and she taught Victor to patrol as she had done for many years. If a rodent was so ill-advised as to dig a hole in any part of the nurseries, she would soon discover it and give notice that its lease was short. Digging frantically around the hole, she barked a series of warnings down the now greatly enlarged opening. Generally the woodchuck decided to move elsewhere.

If the warnings were not heeded, she went into action. Lying quiet but alert under a canopy of squash leaves or some suitable cover, she waited for the intruder to come out of his hole, not just his nose but his whole fat body; then she would pounce on it. Grabbing it by the neck, she would shake it violently, toss it into the air and let it lie where it fell, walking away disdainfully. Victor often wanted to carry the spoil of battle back to the house, but Tom intercepted him and gave the woodchuck a decent burial.

Dawn never was one to instigate trouble, but if a surly dog or an arrogant cat crossed territory that was in every way hers to protect, she never hesitated to make it known. Her firm stance, her deep-chested growl, her tail carried high intimidated interlopers many times her size and settled the matter. And never far from her was Victor, ready to do what she told him to do if that moment came. She met life on her own terms—and death, too.

One morning, after her first early saunter out, with dew still on her nose from where she had thrust it into the grass or under a bush, she went up the stairs slowly, very slowly for one who had been used to taking stairs in a far swifter fashion, but time had been running out for her, and she was no longer agile. She went to Julie's bed and sat beside it, eyes looking up at the beloved face whose eyes were just opening to the new day. Julie reached down to stroke the soft head and murmur her usual morning greeting. A damp paw was placed briefly in her hand, a warm tongue drew itself across the hand; then with a sigh Dawn settled herself down. She crossed her front paws and dropped her head between them; the tail with its white tip quivered.

"Dawn," Julie said gently, placing her hand again on the soft head, but Dawn made no answering move.

That afternoon when they laid Dawn's body

wrapped in her plaid blanket in the grave Tom had dug near a tree in whose shade she had often rested, Victor stood near.

"I think, Tom, that she knew her time had come— animals do. Call it instinct or what you will, but they lend themselves to a wisdom beyond themselves. God tells them in his way, and they try to get the message through to us in their way."

"Dawn always did seem to know just what to do," Tom said, remembering.

"And she did it beautifully."

"Even this."

Julie's eyes were clear as she looked at Tom. "It's incompleteness of life, Tom, that causes grief. Dawn's life was so complete, so fulfilled. I can only be grateful. She was fourteen. That's a long life for a dog."

"And a good life."

Victor standing near them barked. It was his turn now.

Victor

THE YEARS WERE GOLDEN AND THEY WERE PRESIDED over by a golden dog. Victor, in his position now as only dog, had the household and surrounding land as his concern. He divided his time between Tom working among his plants and trees, and Julie as she went about her affairs. He was happiest when he had them both together, sitting in the garden on a summer evening or by the fire when winter settled in. There was an idyllic quality to the days, as if life had reached a plateau where bliss was natural, and time slipped by uncounted. This was the way life had always been; the way it would always be: ten years into twenty years, each one ever more meaningful.

Often in the mail there were letters from families where Dawn's puppies had made homes and names for themselves. An exploit or an adventure always had the true Sheltie ring that made Julie laugh and Tom chuckle. Sometimes the letters brought another kind of news.

"They say they'll never have another dog because there'll never be one like Robin," Julie said as she tucked a letter back into its envelope and handed it to Tom. "Of course, there won't be one like Robin. Each one is an individual, as each human being is, but I hope they won't close the door of their hearts to a new relationship."

"What do you mean?"

"I mean that love comes into life in singular ways, sometimes through an animal, a dear dog."

"Like Victor," Tom reached down to stroke the soft head of the dog who was never far from either one of them.

They were off on their favorite subject, and Julie went on with her theory that animals link one to a whole other way of life.

"I've learned more from them than I've ever taught them," Tom said, "and I credit them with a knowledge different from ours but no less wonderful."

"We think too much!" Julie exclaimed. "An animal responds to something beyond thinking. Look at the way Victor finds a cool place to rest on a hot day, and we push ourselves to work because we feel we've got to get things done."

"I should get back to my cultivating," Tom mused, but he made no move.

Julie's mind, just then, was far from gardens and the work they exacted. "Don't ever shut love out of your life, Tom," she murmured dreamily. "Let it in, no matter how it comes or in what way."

"I'm not apt to as long as I have you." Tom reached out to touch her hand. "What makes you say that, Julie?"

She looked at him, then smiled in reassurance. "That letter we had about Robin and their attitude, that sort of 'never again' point of view."

"I remember when you said you couldn't live without a Sheltie."

"And you said you couldn't live without me!"

"We managed to do both."

"Yes, over many years, nineteen," Tom said.

"Twenty," Julie corrected him, for her way of counting was from the day they met, not the day they were married.

Victor knew that he was not only head of the household but that he had made himself indispensable to it. Julie, with a message to send to Tom at work in garden or orchard, would write it on a piece of paper, tie it to Victor's collar and say, "Take it to Tom," and the message would be delivered. Tom, coming in from work and finding Victor in the house, would say, "Where is Julie?" With a leap and a swift about-turn, Victor would go ahead and lead Tom to where Julie was, then he would bark sharply for recognition. Julie's soft tones and warbling whistle were music to Victor's ears; Tom's hand on his head was total approval. A treat from the special dog box was an extra that he relished.

But his abilities went beyond his activities. He was Julie's protector, becoming more attentive to her as time went on. It went beyond devotion and became a duty he had assigned to himself. Tom, watching him, had an uneasy feeling that Victor knew something, or sensed something, that he did not.

"Don't you think he's almost too watchful, too protective?" Tom asked one day.

"It's his right, Tom. After all, he is the oldest member of this household."

Tom, always surprised by the truth when he didn't want to admit it, said, "How come?"

"It's a simple matter of arithmetic. One year to a human comes close to seven for a dog. Any vet will tell you that. Victor is older by far than either one of us."

Safe in his fifties, Tom felt they were both a long way from another decade. The sixties were as distant as a never-never land.

"Time catches up with us all," Julie remarked, a slight warning tone in her voice. "Remember the story of Canute? He couldn't hold back the tide any more than we can the years."

"A market gardener such as I should certainly know that," said Tom, seeing Julie's point. "I guess the trick is not to be taken unawares, just as you'd try to harvest the best of your crop before frost. Where's Victor?"

"Gone out. Didn't you hear the screen door come to ever so slightly? As long as you're in the house with me, he feels it's all right for him to go off on his own affairs."

"I wonder what he does, where he goes."

For all his attention to the household, Victor did have a life of his own. Ever since his first year and even under Dawn's watchful eye he had the skill to slip away unnoticed. He was there, and then he wasn't there; and his return later was made in the same way. If Tom and Julie were sitting outdoors in the garden, Victor would glide into his place on the grass between their chairs, and they would realize his presence. If they had gone into the house, he would lie quietly on the doorstep until someone thought to open the door. There was never anything apologetic about his manner. He gave no hints as to where he went and what he did, and they asked no questions.

One evening Julie regaled Tom with news that had just reached her.

"Every afternoon Victor goes calling on the Michaels' Sheltie, Meg. That's a mile from here, Tom! I met Mrs. Michaels this afternoon in town, and she told me how much they enjoy our dog, how well mannered he is, and that to see the two of them playing together, then going off on a walk as if they had business of their own to discuss was positively enchanting. She thought we knew."

"Meg? Isn't she worried that something might happen?"

"I asked her about that, but she said Meg was an old dog, ten or so, and that they'd tried for years to breed her without success. Some dogs don't seem meant to be procreators."

"Victor's an old dog, too, but I'm sure he's got plenty of male vigor."

"And Meg has female charm."

Victor seemed to know now that they knew about him, for he no longer slipped off stealthily but strode away in full sight of either Tom or Julie, or both, and his return was made with an air of triumph.

Idyllic as their life had been for many years, there were hints that it would not always be so. Julie's frequent visits to the doctor all that spring, then a week of tests in the hospital, confirmed a fact that had only one word to describe it—*terminal*.

"But we still have the summer, Tom," Julie said, "four whole lovely months of it, and we can be together." She explained what the doctor had said to her. "And, best of all, I can be home, at least for most of the time, with you and Victor."

"And then?"

"Then you'll have Victor."

Everything they could say to each other had been said over the years and over the last few months; now they would live the time that remained. The preciousness of the days was beyond measure. Each one seemed to be part of an eternity that had nothing to do with time. Each one was savored to the full, and cherished.

On a warm August evening when the chirping of crickets came through the open windows, the telephone rang. Tom took the call, and when he returned to the room where Julie was resting on the couch, with Victor beside her on the floor, he was laughing so that he could hardly speak.

"Guess what! That was Mrs. Michaels, and Meg has produced a puppy! They never even suspected she had one in her, but she knew exactly what to do, and she's giving it everything it needs." Tom wagged a finger at Victor, "You old roué, you!"

Julie dropped her hand to rest it on Victor's head. "The line goes on," she said, "Dawn's line. I'm proud of you, Victor. That will give the Michaels a whole new lease on life to have a puppy scampering through their days."

Victor looked from one to the other, thumping his tail.

"But, Julie, they say it's ours, that they don't want a puppy. They say they're too old."

"Oh, never too old!"

"They want us to have her when it is all right for her to leave her mother. Then they are going to have Meg spayed."

Julie laughed. "Tell them to let her be with Meg for four months, Tom. You, know, the usual."

"Four months!" Tom exclaimed. "That will be November."

"Yes, I know."

Julie had been told she had not more than four months to live, and three of them had already gone. The spread of the disease could not be arrested, but the pain had been kept within bounds.

"Bearable bounds," Julie had said one morning to Tom. "I think I can stand anything if I can be at home with you. Home," she smiled up at him as if the loved word gained new meaning.

"What shall we call the puppy?" Tom asked.

Julie did not answer immediately, then she said, "Her name is Nell."

"Why?"

"I don't know why. I just know that is her name."

Four months later, almost to the day, Tom brought Nell home. The house that had become quiet with only an old dog and a man growing older was now filled with a new mirth. Victor knew from the first touching of his cool nose to Nell's small inquisitive one where his responsibility now lay. He had been taking care of humans for a long time, now there was one of his own kind to care for. Shaking himself, he seemed to shed some of his age and took on his new work.

From the start Nell demanded his attention, games were frequent, companionship constant. When tired she would push herself against him, then curl up beside him for a rest. As suddenly restored as she had become exhausted, she would begin tussling him all over again, yipping at his paws, pulling on his tail, until he got himself up and became her playfellow again, running with her as long as she wanted him to.

Victor's demands on her were more subtle. When Tom opened the door as, in deference to Nell it was done more often than usual, both dogs went out. Nell followed Victor a discreet distance from the house, then watched while he showed her what trees were for. She soon caught on, and though she could not do it his way, she made her small puddle nearby. Victor inspected it carefully, reading from it all that he wanted to know about her. Soon she followed him into the shrubbery, and when they emerged, Nell had an air of having attended to her needs and was now more ready than ever for a game. Victor obliged, even though he tired sooner and often returned to the house or sought Tom for protection against her insistent energy.

Nell, in her enthusiasm for the newly discovered

sport of digging, could tear up the earth indiscriminately, but Victor showed her how to dig a hole expertly, drop into it whatever treasure it had taken her fancy to hide, and push the earth back carefully with her nose. There were times when she wanted to repeat the process and unearth the treasure, but Victor would be firm. Once was enough. Stretching himself across the earth, he would remain there until some new ploy called for her attention.

The fact that Nell observed Victor closely and did what he did—or what he wanted her to do—was never more apparent than when food time came and Tom set down their bowls at opposite ends of the kitchen. Nell soon learned that hers was hers and his was his. Her first impulse had been to dash over to Victor's bowl and see what he was having and if it might not be better than what was in her bowl. A low sound, so low that it was almost inaudible to Tom but that made itself clear to Nell, sent her hurrying back to her own bowl. Only after she had licked hers clean, then lapped the floor around it in case a crumb had escaped her, did she cross the room to Victor's. Invariably he left a little something for her.

Excitement ran high when Tom got the car out and Victor clambered up onto the seat beside him. Nell, barking with anticipation, tail waving gaily, eyes bright, leaped up and took her place between them. Looking at Tom and giving his hand on the wheel a quick lick, she turned her eyes toward Victor. Seeing that he was gazing straight ahead, she realized that that was the thing to do and did likewise while her whole body quivered.

Tom had lived with enough families of puppies to know that they were all born with a gladness of being that tended to settle down into the reasonableness of daily life, but with Nell it was something more. It was ecstasy of a high order. Even at the age of a year, when she had filled out to her Sheltie best and had yielded to certain requirements of discipline, she took intense delight in life, even though it was that of a household settled into a somewhat staid pattern. It was Victor more than Tom who had made her well mannered, but it had been accomplished with no loss of her high spirits.

Her markings were those of the true Sheltie; her size and behavior would have won her a blue in any show ring, but she was completely herself. Her mother, Meg, and her grandmother, Dawn, seemed to be as little apparent in her as her father, Victor. She had a prancing gait that made her appear to fly over the ground and a rather shrill bark, which was resorted to when she wanted attention for herself or felt there was someone or something requiring Tom's attention; but the sounds she made most constantly were unlike any Tom had ever heard from a dog. They were joyous warblings, soft little trills, quavers of happiness, all such an inner part of her that they had to find expression.

"You're like a sprite from another world," Tom said to her one day, "but you're all Sheltie too."

Once a customer who came to the house asked Tom if he kept an aviary.

Tom laughed and pointed to Nell. She was running in and out of the shrubbery in a game of her own devising. "She thinks she's a bird."

Chickadees and tree sparrows were darting among the branches with Nell following them. Sometimes they swooped down and tempted her to higher leaps, sometimes they landed on the grass. Nell paused to give them a running start before she went in their pursuit.

"She doesn't seem to want to catch one."

"No, not Nell. This is her game. One of them," Tom amended.

"Like to sell her along with those apple trees I'm buying?"

Tom shook his head. "She's my laughter and my length of days. My other dog is getting old now. I need Nell to see me through."

The customer nodded understandingly.

After he left, Nell came up to the porch to lap water from the bowl that was always there, then settled herself beside Tom.

"It's fun just to be alive, isn't it, Nell?" he said, fondling her. He got her brush and comb and gave her the grooming Julie had always given the dogs every day. He whispered into her ears the praise she reveled in, cocking her head and warming his spirit with the warmth of her brown eyes. She snuggled close to him and took the love he gave her as if there could never be enough. Victor, nearby and half-asleep, watched them. He moved his tail slowly, then closed his eyes. All his movements were slow now, and looking at him, Tom would say inwardly, "Not yet, not yet."

Tom had a dream one night that was as vivid as any waking experience. As the sun brightened his room, he lay still, reliving it. Satisfying and complete, it had an indelible quality to it; he knew it would not fade, as most dreams do, into misty forgetfulness. It would forever be his. To make quite sure that he was really awake, he stretched one arm over the edge of the bed to reach for Victor, who slept, as always, across his slippers. Resting his hand on the long, soft fur of Victor's coat, he felt the measured breathing, the ribs swelling and contracting, the complete relaxation. In a corner of the room Nell slept in her basket, curled up cozily with one paw across her long nose, she had never questioned or tried to preempt Victor's privilege of sleeping by Tom's bed.

"So beautiful, it was so beautiful," Tom murmured,

not loud enough for either dog to hear but to assure himself that he was awake; then he put his head back on the pillow and with eyes wide open relived the dream.

He and Victor were walking together on a sloping green field. Above them the sky was unclouded, and the sun was warm; down the field and not far from where they were standing ran a little brook. The water was clear as crystal, the murmuring it made was musical. Across the brook was an apple tree, and beside it stood a woman. She made no move, but from her lips came a warbling whistle, low but enough to penetrate the stillness and the sound made by the brook. It was a familiar call, but it had not been heard for so long that it brought a leap to Tom's heart. Victor, beside him, pushed against him and looked up at Tom, then he responded to the remembered call. Going across the field to the little brook, he leaped it easily, then ran toward the woman. The two went off together, disappearing into light.

When Tom got up, Victor moved and stretched slowly, then shook himself even more slowly. Tom put his feet into his slippers, warm as they always were from Victor's body. A peace unlike anything he had felt for a long time took possession of him. It was as if he had touched reality, and when reality proclaimed itself, it would be right.

A few days later, in one of his dutiful rough-and-tumble games with Nell, Victor keeled over. Tom reached him while he was still breathing, the tail had its ability to show emotion, the eyes were open, but that was all. There was no need to call the vet. "Go to Julie," Tom leaned over Victor. The eyes flickered and looked into Tom's; then they closed, and the body became still.

Nell came up to sit beside Tom; taking no notice of Victor, she hunched close. And Tom, sitting with one hand on Victor, the other fondling Nell, relived the dream that had prepared him for this moment, the dream that had given life another dimension. In the peace that encompassed him, Tom felt the touch of a paw laid against his cheek. It was so light, so fleeting that he paid no attention to it; then a cold nose was thrust against his face and a warm tongue drew itself down where the paw had touched. He turned to look at Nell. Her eyes were on him, her brown almond-shaped eyes shaded by their light lashes. He stared back at her. Then he held her close to him and buried his head in her long, soft fur. Tears he had wept for Julie came again with the tears he wept for Victor.

Nell freed herself from his clasp. Her tongue found its way over his cheeks. She licked and licked until they were dry.

Nell

IF THE OTHER SHELTIES HAD BEEN GOOD, NELL was even better. Tom had no feeling of disloyalty to Dawn and Victor but rather a sense of privilege that Nell was his. All his. He was aware, as Julie had always been, that each one came into the world with a special gift. Nell had charm that could only be called piquant, and a sparkle, but her special gift was loving. It didn't matter whom, or where; it was something that was her being. Life, to her, was meant for joy; her own first, then others.

All fire and sweetness as she was, she lapped Tom in affection but was quick to tell him if she disapproved of some action of his. Brushing her heavy coat was one thing, combing was quite another, and if he caught a burr, her sharp bark and pulling away told him that it hurt; her jaws would close over his hand that held the comb but her teeth left no impress.

Highly articulate when chasing a stray cat or dog off her property, she was all bounce and gaiety and shrill cries when someone came to her house. That the person had come to see her was obvious, Tom was incidental. Her high sounds of joy made friend or delivery man instantly welcome. When Tom had an errand to do and left her alone in the house for a while, her face was always at the window watching for his return; then once he was seen, her nose was at the door. Sounds of gladness came from so deep within that they were the equivalent of human tears of joy. Collapsing at his feet with tail thumping the floor and tongue lolling, she would look up at him, her eyes saying everything that was in her heart.

"Missed me, little one, didn't you?" He rubbed back of her ears and ran his hand through the deep fur of her chest. "I'll not leave you again unless I absolutely have to, and you know I'll always be back."

It was rare that he left her. No watchdog, she would have greeted an intruder with such a show of affectionate welcome that an intent to harm would soon have been changed into a romp and then a retreat. Generally she went with Tom, sitting demurely in the car and waiting, or at his feet under a table if he attended a

meeting. She was capable of decorum and silence if
such was required.

Her markings were traditional, but there was an ex-
quisiteness about her from white ruff to plumy tail,
slender legs, and dainty paws. She was sturdy of bone
and tough of muscle. A five-mile walk or a day's moun-
tain climb delighted her, but she knew how to conserve
energy. At any stop for rest, she curled herself into
sleep to be ready for the next thrust. She always had a
project. It might be simply digging a deep hole under
a bush to make a cool hollow in which to lie or to
unearth some curious relic with which to play; it might
be cavorting with birds to test her speed against their
flight. The dividing line between project and game was
thin—until a new family moved into a house a short
distance away from Tom, then a project became a responsibility.

Accompanied by Nell, Tom called on the neighbors.
While he talked with Mr. and Mrs. Robbins, Nell devoted herself to two toddlers, whose realm was the
same as hers—the floor. She sat quietly except for the
slow and graceful sweeping of her tail, which indicated
pleasure. She let their small hands explore her; she gave
quick kisses and nuzzled them to their delight. As soon
as one started to crawl away, Nell watched intently,
then crouched along the floor silently, got ahead of the
child and nudged him back to the center of the carpet
and the circle of sunshine where the toys were.

Seeing her maneuver, Tom said, "It's her herding instinct, keeping the flock together."

In a few weeks the family had grown to seven as working mothers left their little ones with Mrs. Robbins for part of the day. Nell was in her element, trotting off to the house as soon as she heard the sound of lively voices and not returning until noon.

Tom went to see Mrs. Robbins and said, "I hope Nell isn't a nuisance. Just let me know and I'll keep her in the house."

"Nuisance! She's better than a helper. As long as she's there, I know the children are safe. She won't let them wander anywhere they shouldn't, and she keeps them all together. I've decided she can count up to seven."

"Of course, she can count! Up to seventy if need be. Trust a sheep dog to know what her flock consists of."

"Look, Mr. Wilson, look at them now. Sometimes I think your Nell tells them stories."

Tom looked to where the children were in a corner of the garden, sitting in a loose circle and watching Nell. Even at a distance the flow of chatter could be heard. Nell's ears flicked in response. One child approached and apparently whispered something to her.

"That's Guy," Mrs. Robbins said. "He won't talk to people, not a word, but he will to Nell, and she listens. Really, Mr. Wilson, I don't know what I'd do without her."

"Nor do I."

To Nell everything was meant to be enjoyed, and every time of year had its fascination. Snow was to be plunged into then rolled in, and the place under the bird feeder where the moles crept out to feast on fallen seed intrigued her. Tom saw her watch a mole intently, then start to approach it. The tiny creature, frozen by panic, seemed unable to move. Nell sat down, put out a paw gently and waited.

Tom, with a snow shovel in his hand, called, "Get it, Nell, get it."

She turned toward him with an expression he had learned to interpret as "Why?" Then she turned back to the small creature and waited patiently until its fright eased and it scuttled ahead to some seed, then back into its hole. Nell snuffled at the snow, then went off a safe distance to have a roll.

Tom, considering the whole procedure, wondered why his instinctive reaction had been to kill something as helpless as it was harmless. Nell's had been to observe something that apparently had as much right to be in the world as she had.

For Nell wind was an unseen force to race with, rain was something to race against as she sought cover from it. Thunder rolling across the sky called to her to look up the way she would at a plane passing overhead or a flight of geese in migration. Planes and birds could be followed with her eyes, but thunder was mysterious and puzzled her, so she challenged it and barked at it. Failing to intimidate it, she let it roll and put her attention on something closer, like a beetle walking across the floor or a fly buzzing by a window.

Tom found that he was observing the life around him more intently because of Nell's interest in it. A grasshopper in the summer fascinated her the way moles had in the winter, and she leaped along beside it in happy copy but not pursuit. A toad called for very close inspection, but a snake was not particularly interesting because it slithered away so quickly and left no scent. The happiest of all her happy times was when she and Tom went for a walk in the woods. It meant crossing a meandering brook. Nell lapped the water, waded into it up to her belly, then talked to it in sharp barks. The brook, running over and around the stones in its bed, talked back to her. Tom went on, cutting across the open field and going toward the woods; he knew that whatever caught Nell's fancy for a while, she would soon leave it and catch up with him. She knew as well as he that the place he was headed for was the place where picnics had often been held. It was an ancient oak, fallen long ago but near the edge of the woods, so that shade could be found if the day was sunny, and the great bole was good to lean against.

In the past he and Julie had often gone there with Dawn and Victor. At the place where roots had been upturned by the tree's fall there had been evidences of woodchuck burrows, but the dogs had never given them more than a passing sniff.

It was years ago that the oak had gone down in a storm. The mass of tangled branches had given shelter to partridges and rabbits, the twigs with any succulence to them had been nibbled by deer. The trunk, gradually going back to the earth from which it had towered, was almost hidden by the ferns growing alongside it. Moss was creeping into decaying crannies. The smell it gave off as the sun bore down on it was good, only a little different from that of sun-warmed earth, which, in the slow circling of time, the tree would become. Tom greeted it as an old friend and cleared a place among the ferns where he might sit down and lean back against the bole.

Half an hour later Nell joined him, giving him a series of quick kisses then flattening herself beside him, panting. His hand found its way across her fur, her back and head seemed warm, her undercarriage was still wet from the brook. She stayed with him long enough to cease panting, then she was off on a project. Tom took a book from his pocket and started to read.

He could hear her digging and realized she was not too far from him. Every now and then she came back to him covered with earth and rotting wood, but she'd give herself a shake and most of it would fly from her coat; only her nose was telltale as she pushed it against him. She snuggled close for a few minutes' rest, then back she went to whatever it was that had her so intrigued. She took time off to share some of the cookies Tom had brought along for their tea, then scampered across the field to the brook to quench her thirst. Tom rarely had so much time to spend in such abandoned fashion, but now after reading awhile, he settled himself into the grass, burrowing his back for the most comfortable contour of the land. And with the sun for a blanket over his legs and his head shaded by ferns, he went to sleep.

The sun was well to the west when Nell came back to stretch out beside him, flat on her side, close to him, wearied but satisfied at last. When Tom awoke, he felt the warmth of her body against him and realized she must have been there a long time. When he reached to stroke her, she lifted her head, then let it drop again.

"Well, whatever you were up to is finished, or you would never have left it, would you, little one?"

Her belly fur was covered with earth mold, her white ruff was dingy, her nails were filled with grit, but she was content. Every inch of her showed it, even the eyes that opened then closed again in blissful sleep. It was clear that she had brought to completion something she had felt compelled to do.

Tom got up slowly, stretched himself, shaking sleep

and stiffness from him. He went to where the oak when it had fallen had upheaved a tumble of stones; this part of the oak was mostly overgrown now and covered with the detritus of the years. Where earth and roots were moist and fresh looking, he saw evidence of Nell's digging. It was a hole so deep that she must have been down it to the length of her tail, obviously in pursuit of something.

Tom knelt and reached into the hole up to his elbows. Digging out more earth, his fingers felt something that was not earth. Reaching in as carefully as if he were an archaeologist on a dig, he brought out the skeletons of two animals that had become linked in some way. Although he handled them tenderly, they came out in far from perfect condition. Some bones broke away at his touch, others crumbled, but skulls and jawbones were intact.

"Tag!" Tom gasped. "Gone to earth in your unending warfare with woodchucks. So, one got you at last, or you got your last one." Studying the remains in his hands, he could see that the woodchuck's teeth had become caught in Tag's collar, a chain one that, though it had rusted, had not rotted as a leather one might have. Tom untangled the chain from the teeth and scraped earth away from the disc that bore Tag's name and his name too.

He stroked the skull. "You always were a scrapper,

Tagalong-too, and you couldn't have gone in a better way, ridding the earth of one more varmint and digging your own grave while you did it." He started to slip the chain into his pocket, then thought better of it and slipped it back over the skull. Reaching again as far as he could down the hole, he pushed in the bones of the woodchuck, then those of Tag. When the skeletons were deeply interred, he filled the hole with earth and mold, packing it tightly, smoothing it, firming it, then covering it all with a flat stone that he found among the chaos of tumbled stones that the roots of the oak had once grasped. He felt reverent as he did it, wondering what might in time grow from soil enriched by two fighters who had met their match not in each other but in death.

Nell was still sleeping when he returned to the place where his book and thermos lay. She opened her eyes and flipped her tail, flicked an ear, and sighed contentedly.

"You've solved a mystery," Tom said to her.

Nell's tail moved again. Compliments always pleased her.

When they started for home, Nell raced merrily across the field, giving not so much as a glance to her excavation. When Tom caught up with her, she was prancing in the brook, talking back to its chatter as only she could.

"What are you going to do next, little one?" he asked her.

She looked at him in a way that said when there was another project, she would follow through on it. Her sleep was deeper than usual that night, and she sought it sooner than Tom did his. He lay awake for a long time wondering what had impelled her to dig among the rotted roots at the base of the old oak.

Tom started making weekly calls on Ben, his room-mate of college days, who was now in the Aurora Nursing Home. Nell went with him. Sometimes they walked, for the distance was not great; sometimes Tom took the car. Ben was confined to a wheelchair, but his mind was as good as ever, if not better. It still took all Tom's wits, and more, to win over him at chess.

"Remember that raggle-taggle dog you had when we were in college, Tom? Whatever happened to her?"

A week ago Tom would have had no answer. Now, thanks to Nell's sleuthing, he could tell Ben Tag's story, going back as it did over many years.

Ben chuckled. "Well, your taste has gone up some. That little Sheltie is a beauty."

"She is, and rare in many ways." Tom reached down to stroke Nell, but she was no longer lying beside his chair. "Nell!" he called conversationally, but there was no answering patter of feet on the linoleum.

"Probably down in the kitchen," Ben suggested.

"No, that wouldn't draw her. She's more likely gone in search of something to do."

"Not apt to find it in a place like this."

"You don't know Nell. Doing for her is finding something that needs to be done. I'll be back soon, Ben, just would like to know what she's up to."

Tom went from room to room. All the people he saw were in their later years. Some, like Ben, looked serene and were reading or finding some small occupation for their hands; others looked vague as if somehow life had slipped beyond their grasp. He asked one of the nurses if she had seen a dog anywhere around. No, she said, then added that she had just come on duty. He saw another nurse and asked the same question.

"Yes, she's been trotting around as if she were looking for someone. I didn't stop her, for she acted as if she knew what she was about. Try the room at the end of the hall. It's a single. The name is Sidway."

The door was wide open, as all the doors were. Tom tapped lightly on the wall before he entered. On a couch by the window sat an old lady, very thin, very erect. There was something glacial about her. Her face looked as if it was used to expressing rebellion, and there was no composure in the tightly set lips. Beside her sat Nell. They were holding hands, paw and hand. Whether Mrs. Sidway could see or hear or even speak,

Tom had no way of knowing. She sat as still as a statue except for the hand that held Nell's paw. Her head was turned slightly toward Nell, as Nell's was to her. They were looking at each other and quite clearly communicating.

Nell, aware of the presence in the doorway, turned to face Tom. A flick of an ear, a quiver of the long tail that hung over the edge of the couch acknowledged him, but everything in her seemed to ask him not to interrupt. So Tom turned away and went back to Ben's room.

"She's sitting with a Mrs. Sidway who looks frozen in immobility, but I guess Nell knows what she's doing."

"Well, if Nell can get through to Mrs. Sidway, she's doing more than anyone has been able to do for a long time."

Ben told Tom the story of a brilliant, wealthy woman for whom the problems of the years had become prison bars. "Why for her more than anyone else, who can say," Ben went on. "We're all old here, and we've all got problems. She used to be the life of the place, then her memory began to go back on her. When she couldn't recall what she wanted to say, she got annoyed with herself, then angry at the rest of us, and bitter. She doesn't talk to anybody now. I used to wheel down the hall to see her, but I haven't for a long time."

"She must be lonely, shut up in herself like that."

Ben nodded. "It's as if she'd locked some kind of door in her mind and deliberately lost the key."

An hour later Tom went down the hall to Mrs. Sidway's room. A nurse followed him and stood just behind him in the doorway.

The position of the two on the couch had changed only to the extent that Nell's head was on Mrs. Sidway's lap, and the woman's hand was resting on the dog's head. Neither was asking anything of the other, but each was giving something to the other. Small sounds like little sucking whispers were coming from lips pressed less tightly together; subdued whimpers came from Nell as she lifted her cool black nose to those lips and drew her tongue swiftly across them.

Behind Tom the nurse said in a low voice, "Her minister, her doctor, all of us here, have tried to reach her with some kind of stimulation, but she won't pay any attention. Your little dog is giving her something that she needs."

Tom spoke gently, "Nell, it's time to go."

Nell looked toward him, then she reached up again to place a kiss on the pale, lined cheek. She came slowly down from the couch, stretched, shook, and crossed the room to stand beside Tom.

Mrs. Sidway looked at Tom with eyes that clearly saw him. "Please bring your dog with you next time you come." Her tone was imperious, as of one accustomed to being obeyed, but it was polite.

Tom, startled, murmured an affirmative. As he went down the hall, the nurse followed him to the door, amazement was large on her face. "Those are the first rational, civil words I've heard that woman speak since I came here two years ago."

Some children were playing on the lawn outside the Aurora, and Nell would gladly have joined them, but Tom was firm about it's being time for them both to go home.

Once in the car, he put an arm around Nell and hugged her close to him as she sat on the seat beside him. "You're a seeing-heart dog, Nell. You knew what that old lady has been hungering for, and you gave it to her."

Nell looked away from Tom and toward the road. Her attitude was slightly smug, as if she had done what needed to be done and further comment was unnecessary.

A pattern had been established. Nell went with Tom on all his visits to the Aurora, sat beside him and Ben for a polite while, then trotted off on her rounds. The nurses enjoyed reporting about her. "She seems to seek out the loneliest, the most inarticulate, the ones who sit looking vaguely into space hour after hour, and conveys something to them. There are a few who brush her away, and she knows not to bother them, but she always ends up with Mrs. Sidway."

"Do you suppose Mrs. Sidway gives her any tidbits?" Tom asked reluctantly, knowing that Nell had never been one to accept a bribe.

"I'm quite sure not," the nurse replied. "Mrs. Sidway hasn't any little stores that we know of, and besides, there would be telltale crumbs."

"Nell is a very tidy eater."

The nurse still shook her head. "Mrs. Sidway gives your little dog the only thing she has to give—undivided attention—and your dog gives her love."

"I guess that's what Nell came into the world with a good supply of."

All through the winter and into the spring the weekly visits continued. Before them Nell received a special brushing so that her coat shone, and she fairly danced with excitement when Tom called her into the car; she apparently knew exactly where they were going.

"How old is Nell?" Ben asked.

"Five, this year."

"She's done a lot to make people happy."

"And herself most of all," Tom added. "I've never known anyone, animal or human, to enjoy life as much as she does."

"I'm glad she's so young. She's got years and years ahead of her."

"Right, by the usual reckoning she's just coming into her prime. But if you asked Nell, she'd probably say, 'What's time got to do with it anyway?' She always manages to have the last word."

The children playing on the lawn called to Nell when they saw her come out of the Aurora with Tom and start toward the car. With her prancing steps she ran toward them, tail wagging; the gay little sounds of joy she could make so well were a series of short happy barks. Tom watched, pleased by the way Nell could swing so quickly from her dignified behavior with the people in the home to her play with a group of children.

"Here, Nell, catch!"

One of the boys picked up a wooden croquet ball and threw it toward her.

Nell, delighted at being part of their game, leaped high, mouth open to catch the ball. She didn't catch it, but it caught her on the side of the head, then it fell to the ground. Nell stood still, her tail drooped, her ears went back, her body quivered. She reached out to paw at the ball as if to retrieve it, but her paw couldn't find the ball, and slowly she crumpled down beside it.

Tom had seen it all and ran to pick her up. The children crowded around him.

"She isn't hurt, is she?"

"No, I think not. Just dazed. She'll be all right, but don't ever play with a wooden ball with a dog. Even if she'd caught it, it could have cracked her teeth."

They walked to the car with Tom, saying they were sorry, reaching out to stroke Nell. By the time Tom placed her on the seat, she was struggling to sit up, and by the time he had started the motor, Nell had found her voice and was barking back at the children in answer to their waving hands.

Once they got home, Tom felt her over carefully and was certain she was as sound as ever. He gave her an extra piece of meat in her dinner and had a gentle rough-and-tumble game with her on the lawn before bedtime. He knew she was sturdy, but it took a long time for him to shake off the thought that life itself is fragile.

The incident, frightening as it had been momentarily, was forgotten as the days went on. Nell visited the Robbins's house every weekday morning and took her charge of the children; twice a week now in the afternoon she and Tom went to the Aurora; the rest of the time she followed her own pursuits or kept Tom company wherever he went, whatever he did. The summer days called for being outdoors, for taking walks, and Tom scarcely missed a day going down to the brook. Nell danced happily along the edge, pattered through the water, scooping it up with her nose, then running to catch up with him. Tom was glad that she had so much capacity to entertain herself, for he tired easily now and was more willing to sit down with a book than search out the longer trails. But the trail that led up to the hemlock stand was never too long. Tom followed it for the memories it brought, and Nell for the smells that intrigued her. There was a special flat rock where Tom liked to sit and rest. Nell, returning from an exploration of her own, would give him a quick kiss, then settle down beside him in complete acceptance of his quieter style of life.

The first time it happened, Tom attributed it to a bad dream and thought little of it.

He was wakened out of sleep one night by a curious sound and, putting on the light, saw that Nell had fallen out of her basket and was lying on one side on the floor, her legs moving as if she was running in a race. Quickly he got out of bed and knelt beside her, smoothed his hand down her back and said her name repeatedly. Soon the running action ceased, and she lay still for a moment, then raised her head and looked at him. Her expression seemed to say, "Where exactly was I?" He got her some warm milk with a little sugar in it. She lapped it eagerly, then went around and around the bowl cleaning it. Satisfied that there was no more, she gave herself a good shake, returned to her basket, and went promptly back to sleep.

By morning it seemed that it had been as much of a dream to Tom as to Nell, but there was her bowl on the floor, and there must have been a reason for him to have given her food in the middle of the night.

Two weeks later, while doing some work in the garden one afternoon, Tom heard a strange sound. It was like crying. He knew Nell's voice well enough to recognize it, but he had never heard it other than in excitement or joy. He found her on the grass near the house. Her body was stiff and taut, her legs were thrashing violently, her eyes were glazed, her mouth foaming. He knelt beside her and spoke her name. When the storm had passed and she was limp and calm, he carried her into the house, wiped her with a damp cloth, and gave her some milk. In a short while she was her usual self, ready for a game, ready to go calling.

The call they made was to the veterinarian.

Tom told the story as he had observed it in Nell's behavior. The vet asked several questions as routine as those asked by a medical man. He knew Nell as he had known her father, Victor, and heard legendary tales of her grandmother, Dawn. Her heritage was good, her care had been the best. The vet asked, "Has she ever received a blow on the head?"

Tom's first thought was no, then he remembered the croquet ball.

The vet examined her more closely, much to Nell's delight because this gave her a chance to draw her tongue across his face, and she quivered with the joy she felt at any tender contact.

"Let's have an X ray," the vet said quietly.

With new knowledge, the vet informed Tom that there had unquestionably been some damage to the skull; only time would reveal the extent. "She will be subject to convulsions, and they will be unpredictable. She might have one tomorrow and not another for three months."

"And . . ." Tom couldn't ask the rest of his question.

"There will be a day when one will be more than she can survive."

"Isn't there anything I can do for her, any treatment?"

"If you love her."

"Love her!" Tom exclaimed while his thoughts raced to all the others who loved her, too.

"There is medication to control it. If she has suffered brain damage, there is, as yet, no cure."

Tom saw the future in the veterinarian's eyes.

When he left the office, it was with a bottle of pills and instructions how to administer them. The vet laid his hand on Tom's shoulder, patting it gently. Nell, sprightly as ever, danced happily out of the office and toward the car.

It was midsummer. Tom was relieved that no visits to the Robbins's were on Nell's calendar, for the children were all away. He was eased, too, that at the Aurora most of the patients were moved out to the garden for the long afternoons, and Nell could make her round of visits with his watchful eye upon her. He had learned much during the past weeks. When she came and pressed herself close to him, he knew an attack was imminent. Generally he could get her home or into a quiet place where it would not alarm others and she could not harm herself.

For weeks she would be free of any trouble—gay, fun loving, love giving, her coat shining, her eyes sparkling. Tom often watched her waltzing across the field, playing with the wind then coming back to snuggle up to him when he took a rest as if she thought she could keep one side of him warm. He began to hope that her sturdy frame, her joy in life, her age, which entitled her to many more years, would prove able to help her overcome the threat.

October's gold came early and lasted long, and for one whole week Tom decided to do nothing but revel in it. The time was a quiet one in the nursery business, and what tasks he still did could be done by his helpers, who were as much his partners now as he had been to his father many years ago.

"I'm taking the week off," he announced one morning, "not going anywhere, just doing something different every day."

That was one of the advantages of getting into one's sixties—being able to do what you liked, when you liked, and for as long as you liked. Nell, seeing a picnic basket being put together, realized something of what was in store and willingly set aside her current project or self-imposed duty to give herself completely to Tom. It was like a little honeymoon for the two of them, and during that week of day after sunny day with leaves falling around them they did all their favorite things.

One day Tom took his fishing tackle and went to a nearby lake, where a canoe was his for the asking. He was not intent on getting any fish but on paddling over the water stained red and gold as it reflected the leaves from trees along the shore. Sometimes he did not even paddle but lazed along the water. Nell was enchanted by all she saw. She had long known that a canoe was no place for frolicking, and her stillness matched the day. Often she flattened herself out and went to sleep, but more often she watched intently. If anything moved in the woods or if a beaver's dark head broke the smooth surface with a v of ripples streaming out behind the flat tail, she'd stiffen and watch more intently but would make no move.

They also had long, leisurely walks through the field and in the woods. Nell raced the leaves that floated in the air, rolled in ones that had come to ground, and was so much in color like them that Tom often lost sight of her. The brook challenged her more than ever as it carried away its cargoes of leaves. Nell rushed into the water, ducked her head under the leaves, talked back

to them and then came leaping out, shaking herself.
Several times they went up to the hemlock stand. The
quiet green of the trees came as a contrast to the shout-
ing radiance of the world of colored leaves. The needle-
covered ground made no sound as they walked over it.
When Tom reached the flat rock and leaned against it
for a rest, Nell settled beside him and became as much
a part of the green silence as she had been of the bright
glory of rustling leaves.

On Saturday they went off to climb a small hill where
Tom and Julie had often gone in midsummer to pick
blueberries. No blue freight was on the bushes now,
only the red of leaves and the brown of bare branches.
The hill leveled off to a wide, flat area, a sort of moorland where bracken and yellowed grasses waved in the
light wind. There were outcroppings of granite, clumps
of white everlastings, and sweet fern gone brittle but
that still left a fragrance on hands that rubbed it. Nell
raced ahead; whether pursuit on a scent was real or
imagined it was all in fun. She darted after a covey of
partridges, who were safe with their wings. She stood
transfixed beside Tom as he watched a flock of migrat-
ing geese go over.

When Tom found the perfect hollow in which to sit,
with a sun-warmed boulder to lean back against, he
settled down and brought out their picnic. Nell snuggled beside him and took her share, a handful of small

biscuits that disappeared quickly. She sighed contentedly, crossed her front paws, sunk her head into them,
and went to sleep. Tom laid his hand on her head and
let his eyes range across the waving grasses and faded
remnants of summer to the distant hills. All around him
was beauty that spoke of the long warm season of growing and fruition, but the fading grasses hinted of winter
to come.

Nell lifted her head and looked at Tom. It was a
curious glance, as if she wanted to fix him in her mind
just as he was at that particular moment.

"What are you thinking about, little one?" He returned her gaze, admiring the slender nose with its
moist black tip, the smooth golden head, the warmth in
the brown eyes; but there was more than warmth he
realized. There was a sagacity he could not interpret,
for at that moment she seemed to know so much more
than he did.

She dropped her head onto her paws and went back
to sleep. Tom, with his hand resting on the warm fur of
her body, closed his eyes, but not to sleep. He felt happiness deep within him, like a vein of gold running
through the ore of daily living. It seemed to have no
beginning, it could not have an end: it always was and
would be. He thought back over the days, one by one.
It was as if the best of life had been encapsulated into
a week.

And so it had.

That night Nell went into a series of convulsions. When one ceased and Tom comforted her, it took her longer than usual to regain her equilibrium. Soon she would collapse into another. The violence almost seemed to tear her apart. Tom spoke her name, he called, he shouted, but nothing reached her. The glazed eyes held no recognition, the tail and ears were all part of the storm that raged through her and made no response except convulsively. There was nothing Tom could do but sit beside her, hoping his presence gave her something. And the hours crept by. The vet had warned him this would happen sometime, and Tom knew, when the first gray light preceding morning came, that he faced a future without Nell.

He lifted the body, stilled beyond all tumult, and laid it in her basket, then covered it with the tartan that had been her blanket since puppy days. He threw himself down on his bed, too ravaged to think, too exhausted to weep. When the full light of day came, he would do what had to be done.

He had not thought he could sleep, but he must have, for he was wakened by a dream—a dream so bright in its color, so warm in its glow that he lay still in the aura it gave him. It was like that other dream of the green hill, the crystal stream, and the blue, blue sky, only this dream was all tawny and gold.

A girl came running toward him, so young she had only just grown out of childhood. Her dress was made of an old-fashioned print, the square cut of the neck showed her strong shoulders; her arms were bare and suntanned; her feet were bare, and the sound they made was a rustling sound; her shoulder-length hair, tossed in the breeze of her running, was only a little more golden than her skin. Her eyes were brown, so warmly brown. She was not smiling, but her face was suffused with joy. Lissome and lithe, her appearance was that of one who had been set free. She was all of life: life running to meet life.

"But I don't know you," Tom said as she approached him.

She ran past him into a light that was not the sun flooding his room but a light so dazzling that he closed his eyes against it. In that moment he lost her; and knew.

He lay still for a long time, feeling that his fingers held a golden thread. However long he lived, however old he grew, with failing sight and diminished hearing, this he would see with all its intensity of color, this he would hear—the rustling of feet in their swift passage.

The earth yielded easily to his shovel, and Tom went down a good depth. Wrapped in her blanket, with her ball and her leash, for there would never be another dog, he laid the body down tenderly. All he could think as he put the earth over it were long-forgotten lines of Emily Dickinson's—"and best must pass through this low arch of flesh."

Later that morning he walked the short distance to tell Mrs. Robbins about Nell. She knew by his look and by the fact that no eager little four-footed friend danced beside him that something had happened. She took both his hands in hers. There were no words. All she might say was in her eyes.

"But how do I tell the children?" Tom asked.

"Just as the plain words come to you. They have their way of facing reality. Philip told them yesterday that his grandfather had gone to heaven. They knew what he meant."

Tom went to the garden and found the children playing in the sandbox. At sight of him they looked up. He spoke quickly before any questions could be asked. "Nell was very sick last night. She didn't see the morning."

There was silence.

"You mean she's gone to heaven?"

Tom nodded.

Silence again and small fingers dribbling sand through them. Then Philip started to smile. His small, round face looked like a rising sun with the light that beamed through it. "Now I know my grandfather won't be lonely in heaven, for he'll have Nell to play with."

Guy shook his head solemnly. "Nell's going to be awfully busy. She'll have so many children to take care of. Here she had just us."

Then they went back to their play.

That afternoon Tom went to the Aurora, and he went directly to see Mrs. Sidway. She was sitting on the couch, reading. Standing in the doorway, Tom realized that the glacial look that had gone from her face some months ago had not returned. She had the appearance of any very old person who was wearied by time and waiting for release. He tapped softly on the door frame as he had always done. She looked up from her book. Seeing him and smiling faintly in recognition, she said, "Come in."

Tom crossed the room and stood beside her. Words failed him.

"Sit down," she gestured to a near chair, "please." Her tone was courteous. When he was seated, she said, "You don't need to tell me that something has happened. The last time I stroked Nell's glossy head and we looked into each other's eyes, I had a fleeting sense that we were saying farewell. It seemed then an odd quirk of my mind, but apparently it was not."

They talked together for a while, and when Tom got up to leave, Mrs. Sidway took his hand. "You'll come to see me sometimes, when it is seasonable for you?"

"Yes, of course, I'll come every week."

A smile trembled on her pale lips. "That will give me something to look forward to."

Tom was halfway down the hall when he heard her calling him. He went back to her room.

She pointed a finger at him. "Don't live in memory. That's where I made my mistake. Cherish it, but don't live in it."

When he got home, he tidied the house that had had little attention during the past week, in order to give himself something to do. He put Nell's things away, the basket, the water bowl, the dish. The house was full of reminders of the dogs that had raced through it, whose home it had been. There were the corners where they had slept, the rug where a patch of sunshine had always been preempted; the easy chair appropriated by one after another no matter what the deterrent. He and Julie had given up at last and called it the dog chair. There was scarcely a piece of furniture that did not bear some marks of puppy teeth or a rug that did not have at least one frayed corner. Tom could see them all —and remember—and smile; but it was Nell he saw most of all, and he could not smile. He could only wince as he felt her loss closing in around him like a wall.

He thought of the people at the Aurora and of others like them in other homes. He was more fortunate, still with much of his old strength and able to carry on for himself, but he could not escape the loneliness that nibbled at the edges, then gnawed at the core of his being. Yet life went on, and somehow a way was found to go on with it until the fullness of time came. For Nell there had been no such fullness, and yet the thought that took possession of his anguish was that perhaps she had accomplished what she had come into the world to do. She had given love without measure or deserving. It had been her gift, her golden gift, and he would fail her if he let it tarnish.

What was it Julie had said to him once, "Don't ever shut love out of your life, Tom. Let it in, no matter how it comes or in what way."

Una

Snow came early that year, almost as soon as the leaves had fallen and been blown or raked away, whitening the ground and giving the countryside a different look. It was a light snow, right for revealing tracks of birds and small animals. Tom went to the woods. In the loneliness that gripped him he took comfort in the tracks, knowing that others had been the way he was going. The tracery left by a partridge, the lacelike imprint of a meadow mouse, the swift impress of a fox, all told him he was not alone.

Then, one November afternoon on his way up to the hemlock stand, he saw footprints left by a human being. Someone had entered the woods on a trail that came in from the east and that joined up with the path he took so often. He studied the mark of boots with heavy rubber soles, so much smaller than his own that a footstep placed over one obliterated it. Whoever it was had walked slowly and deliberately, for the marks were so uniform; then, left of the prints but parallel with them, were those of a dog, a large dog, for the paws had come down heavily in the snow.

Tom was puzzled. Nell might have kept pace with him for a short distance, but soon she would have been off after a scent or to give herself a roll. Dashing back, she would have hurled herself against him with a shrill and joyous caroling. He would have agreed with her that early snow was fun to play in and with, far better than the deep snows that came later. Now he bent down to study the paw prints that were so evenly spaced, so measured. There was another walker with a companion in the woods. Before he reached the flat stone, the tracks veered off on one of the lesser used trails and disappeared.

This happened again and again. Sometimes the tracks looked so freshly made after a light snow that Tom felt sure he would overtake the walkers, but he did not, and he had no desire to follow them out of the woods. For many years he had enjoyed the deep quiet of the hemlock stand; if another felt to do likewise he would not intrude. One day at the flat stone where he often rested, he saw that the walker had brushed away the snow on it and had sat there; close by was the mark

of the dog's haunches. A mitten was lying on the far side
of the stone. Tom picked it up and examined it. It was
too small to fit his hand, and it was machine made, not
like the ones Julie had made for him of natural wool and
with intricate patterns.

Feeling as if the first few words in a conversation had
been uttered, Tom was seized with an idea to continue.
He found a stick on which he mounted the mitten se-
curely and put it in the snow near the stone; then he
found another stick. With a stub of pencil and a scrap
of paper from his pocket he scribbled a message: *Who
are you and where do you come from? We both walk in
the woods so often, it would be nice to meet. T. Wilson
(South Road).* He stuck it in the snow back of the stone,
low down so it would not blow away but still could be
seen.

The next day when he went to the woods, the mitten
was gone. The stick on which it had been impaled was
lying on the ground, but the scribbled message had not
been touched, nor had any words been added to it. Tom
felt the way he sometimes did when a telephone con-
nection was cut off and he'd find he was talking to
himself. Sitting on the stone where the other had sat,
he reached his left hand into the hollow where the dog
had sat. He could almost feel their presence. He tried
to picture who the two might be, but he could bring no
image to mind.

And then, walking earlier than usual one afternoon, Tom came upon them. He was striding along in the quiet that even a light snow gives to the air, heading for the flat stone, when he saw them. He stood still. No words came to him, no shout of salutation, but his eyes took in the scene and, like the pieces of a puzzle, it all came together, and the picture was there.

A boy was sitting on the stone. Tom could not see his face, for he was looking in the direction ahead. Beside him was a big dog, a German Shepherd wearing a harness to which a U-shaped handle was affixed. The dog turned toward Tom but made no move. The pointed ears went back then forward; the tail made a slight sweep over the snow; the head reached a long muzzle toward the boy's face; the tongue started licking. Even at a distance Tom could hear the subdued sounds the dog was making. He could almost feel the warmth of the tongue, and something within him ached.

"What is it, Una? A squirrel?" The boy looked back over the way they had come, facing Tom.

The dog put one paw on the boy's knees.

"All right, Una, but let's stay here a little while longer, then we'll go."

Face to face as they were, Tom could not speak, nor did he want to intrude on the intimacy of a boy and a dog in the silence of a woodland. He moved back a few steps, then retraced his way home. An unseeing boy and a seeing dog, that was what the two sets of foot-prints said; that was why the mitten had been taken but the note had gone unread. "Tomorrow," Tom told him-self, "I'll go at this same time and make myself known."

Without the snow there would have been no tracks with a story, whose hint Tom had not taken but whose meaning now was clear. He respected the dog who, though she had seen Tom, had paid no attention to him. The boy was her concern, and she had nothing to do with anything or anyone else. For the first time in many weeks, Tom went to bed impatient for the next day.

A warming trend had set in, and much of the snow had run off, but Tom needed to follow no footprints to the familiar flat stone. As he drew near, he began to walk more slowly. And there they were, just as on the previous day, but the boy's head was in his hands, his hands were on his knees, and his shoulders were shak-ing. Tom stood still: yesterday he had not wanted to intrude on solitude, today he felt loath to intrude on sorrow. Another time, he thought, and started to turn back. But the dog swung her head toward him and held him in her gaze.

Tom had had dogs for enough years to be able to read something in their expressions. This dog was not asking but imploring him to do something—the large round eyes, the pointed ears moving back then forward, the paw laid on the boy's shoulder, all had meaning. The dog looked away from Tom and at the boy, then back at Tom. Tom started to whistle softly, no particular tune but a sound that would announce the presence of another in the hemlock stand. If the boy looked up, Tom told himself, he would stop; if not, he would go on his way, knowing no intrusion was wanted.

The boy looked up and put one hand on the dog's head. The way it turned gave him direction, and he faced Tom.

"Hello," Tom said, moving forward and sitting down on the flat stone beside the boy. "Mind if I join you for a while?"

The dog shifted so that Tom could sit close to the boy, and Tom did what he had seen her do with her paw. He placed his hand on the boy's knees. The boy, feeling the hand, put his own over it. The gesture became a handshake. The boy murmured something, but speech was not easy for him just then. Tom did the talking, saying enough about himself so that the boy would feel he knew him, saying it in such a way that he hoped the boy would know that he cared. "So, you might as well call me Tom even though I'm old enough to be your grandfather."

Tears had left no mark on the boy's face, but distress had. Now his expression began to change. Something like a smile quivered over his lips. "I've always wanted to have a grandfather. My name is Gareth."

"There must be a reason for such a special name."

"There is, my hands! Remember Sir Gareth, one of King Arthur's knights? His hands were 'large, fair and fine.' My mother said when I was born that was all she could think of, for my hands were so big." He splayed them out on his knees. "She didn't know how useful they would be to me—my hands and Una."

At the sound of her name, Una sought the boy's face and lapped it with her long tongue. He stroked her and said softly, "Rest now, Una." She eased her body down slowly, front legs straight, long nose sunk on them. The air was warm, the woods were quiet. Two who had newly found each other began to fill in the spaces of the past.

Gareth spoke with a simple directness as he told the story of the automobile accident that had taken his parents' lives and his sight. "I was six years old, and I'm seventeen now, but I can see them clearly in my mind. I always will." He had spent a long time in hospitals, but though the broken body had been repaired, the eyes could not be saved. He had been sent to a school for the blind and had mastered the skills that would serve for sight. A year ago, the summer before he entered public high school, he had obtained a Seeing Eye dog and had spent a month in training with her. His words came to an end, but Tom knew the story had not. It was for none of what Gareth had said in a matter-of-fact way that he had been weeping.

"Where do you live?" Tom asked.

"At Herndon. Mr. and Mrs. Banneker are my guardians. I've been with them only a month. They're the third family set up to take care of me. I won't be on my own until I'm eighteen, and that won't be until next summer."

"But Herndon, that's a—" then Tom caught himself.

The boy nodded. "That's the trouble. Trailers are small, and at the park they're packed together like sardines in a tin." Gareth turned full face to Tom, and the woe that had gone from his expression returned. "Mr. Banneker says I can't keep Una."

"But what would you do without her?"

"It's not that. What would she do without me? Who'll take care of her?" Speaking was difficult, and Gareth fought to gain control of his words. "She's special, she's a person."

Tom again laid his hand on Gareth's knees, the other ran over Una's back, the wiry dark coat so different in feel from the silkiness of that of the Shelties.

"Mr. Banneker said I would have to take her to the vet to—"

Gareth felt the pressure of Tom's hand and knew that he did not have to say what he could not find words for.

After a silence, Tom asked, "Why is it so urgent?"

"Because they're leaving, and the trailer isn't big enough for all of us. Una goes into a very small space under a table, but"—he struggled for words—"I could send her back to the Seeing Eye for assignment for another blind person, but I'll need her again, I just know it. If I could only find a temporary home for her."

They talked until the sun lost warmth in its lowering and the short November day began to close in. Una stood up, stretched, then pushed herself against Gareth. He took her head in his hands and said her name softly, then he faced Tom. "Una is telling me it's time to go."

"How much longer will you be around, Gareth?"

"Until the end of the week. Mr. Banneker is heading for a construction job in the Southwest, in Arizona. He wants me to learn the trade, thinks I'll be good because of my hands, but I'll finish high school first wherever he settles."

"And what do you want to learn?"

"I want to be a lawyer."

"What does Mr. Banneker say to that?"

"He laughs, says I'll be lucky to finish high school and that there's not a chance of my going to college. But I will, somehow I will."

Una was pushing herself harder against Gareth, putting herself so that he could place his left hand on her harness. She was in charge and expected to be obeyed.

Tom grasped the right hand held toward him. "We'll meet here tomorrow?"

Gareth smiled. It was the first time Tom had seen

light in his face. "Yes. Thanks a lot. Yes. Una, forward, that's a good girl."

Tom watched them go off briskly. They followed the path for a few yards, then took a lesser trail and soon disappeared from his sight.

Once home, Tom had errands to do that included his weekly call at the Aurora. Usually he spent an hour or so with Ben and looked in on Mrs. Sidway briefly, but this time he found them both in Mrs. Sidway's room playing chess. She looked up as he entered.

"Aren't you rather late?"

"The days are getting short. It's dark so much earlier."

"That's not the reason."

"No, it's because I met a young man in the woods, and we got into conversation."

Tom told them of his encounter with Gareth and Una and something of the story behind it all.

"Interesting," Mrs. Sidway said.

Tom wondered if she had really heard anything, for her eyes had never left the chessboard, and in a series of swift moves she took Ben's remaining rook. Tom rose to go. Ben was still immersed in the game, and Mrs. Sidway barely looked up. But Tom was not out of the room when she said, "Come soon again and bring that dog with you."

That dog!

The evening was neither warm nor cold, so Tom lit

a fire on the hearth, pulled his chair up to it and brought
his supper tray before it. He had often dropped his left
hand to rest on Nell's back as she sat beside him. He had
not done it for several weeks, but this time he did, just
to see what it would feel like, just in case. He had shut
his mind to the thought of ever having another dog, and
something in his heart had shut too. He was thinking
differently now, and the more he thought, the more
reasonable it all seemed. When Gareth had said,
"Who'll take care of her?" Why had he not answered,
"I will." Una needed a home; he needed a friend. It was
as simple as that.

Gareth had been faced with an ultimatum, and time
was running out. Tom went to the telephone, wondering if people who lived at Herndon had phones. He
found the name Banneker in the book and dialed the
number. The voice at the other end was gruff, but it
softened as Tom introduced himself and said he had
met Gareth when walking in the woods.

"Want to speak to him?"

"No, just tell him I've found a home for his dog."

"That all?"

"I'll tell him more about it tomorrow."

"That's better news for the Missus and me than it will
be for him. We never did like dogs, but we had to take
this one along with the boy. But we can't keep her
when we leave here, and that's day after tomorrow."

When Tom went back to sit by the fire, he had the

feeling from Mr. Banneker's tone that he would have been as glad to part with Gareth as he was with Una.

The cheerful sound of whistling drew Tom as he approached the flat stone in the hemlock stand. Gareth was whittling a piece of wood, whistling as he worked. Una was nearby but free. Her harness lay against the stone. She came running to meet Tom, then trotted back with a springy step to stand beside Gareth. When Tom sat down on the stone, Gareth told him he was making a whistle for him to use with Una.

"Gareth, she's got her head on my knees. She's looking up at me with those big eyes almost as if she knew me, as if she knew we were going to be friends."

"Of course, she does. I've told her all about you."

"You mean she knows she's going to be mine for a while?"

Gareth laughed and shook his head. "Oh, Tom, you've got it all wrong. You don't know anything about a dog like Una. She's not yours. You're hers. For a while, until I get back."

Tom was puzzled.

"It's a very special relationship. We look at each other, and she tells me things the way I tell her things."

"No words?"

"Not many."

Tom thought he knew about dogs, but for the next half hour he listened intently as Gareth told him about Una: her feeding at regular times, light in the morning and a proper meal in the late afternoon, her grooming every day, her need for exercise.

"There are three words that sum up her training, and they're important all through her life—firmness, praise and love. If you want her to do something, she must do it, then you praise her for it as if it were the most wonderful thing in the world; and you give her love, great gobs of it all the time." Gareth laughed, "You'll get it back, too."

"Does she ever have to be reprimanded? I can't imagine it."

"Oh, yes, she's human just like everyone else. If you do need to scold her, you use the bad word." Gareth spelled it carefully so that Una would not think he was saying it, "P-H-O-O-E-Y. You sort of spit it out, but never use it unless she does something—" Gareth paused, "well, something she shouldn't do."

Tom nodded.

"She knows all the usual words that a trained dog learns, and she'll pick up new ones from you. You'll get on to her signals, just as she will to yours."

"What's she like with other dogs?"

"If she's working, like when I have her in harness or

when you have her with you in your car, she'll ignore them. If she's free, the way she is now, she'll be friendly and have a game or two with them, but she should come to you as soon as you call her back. Like this—" Gareth put the wooden whistle he had been making to his lips and blew through it. The shrill sound penetrated the silence.

Una looked up from the nosing she had been doing, then she came bounding back to sit before Gareth and place both paws on his knees, tilting her head to know what was expected of her. Her chain-link collar hung loosely. Gareth reached into his pocket for a short leash. He snapped an end to the ring from which her license and rabies tag hung, then handed the other end to Tom. "Here, and I think it's time for you both to go."

"What about her harness?"

"She won't wear it with you. It would only confuse her because she knows you can see. I'll keep it with me until we meet again."

Tom felt like an actor in a play, for what was taking place was high drama, but the other actors knew their lines better than he did his. "When will that be?"

"Next summer, when I'm eighteen. I'll be on my own then. Tom, could I stay with you then, work around your place until I get a job? I hope to earn enough money to get to college."

"That's what I'd like for us all."

Contentment wrote itself across Gareth's face. "Thanks," he said, opening his hands and holding them out as if the more-than-thanks that he could not find words for were in them.

Una sensed something was happening and pawed playfully at Gareth while a a subdued singing sound came from deep within her chest. Gareth reached for the special, rather long cane lying beside the stone. He stood up, with the cane hanging over his right arm, the harness swinging loosely from his left hand. "I feel I can stand up to anything now," he said, "knowing Una will be cared for and that I'll be coming back to you both."

"We'll walk with you through the woods."

Gareth shook his head. "No, I'm all right. Before I got Una I had mobility training at school, and with this cane I can go anywhere, but it isn't so much fun as walking with Una because I can talk to her. Just tell her to come, and she'll go along with you. She knows. If she dillydallies, tell her to heel and jerk the leash a little."

Tom reached for Gareth's hand and closed his around it. "She'll have the best of care and all the love I can give her."

Gareth was smiling. "You're like a dog, Tom, you don't ever say too much."

Tom realized it was the highest compliment Gareth could give him, and his pressure on the hand increased.

"Now, go," Gareth said.

Tom jerked on the leash. "Una, come." He used the low, commanding tone Gareth had told him was the most effective.

Una's head went up in surprise. She looked first at Tom, then back at Gareth. Tom started walking, repeated firmly the word *heel* and drew on the leash. Una fell into step beside him. Once or twice she hesitated and tried to pull back, then accepted the fact that direction was being given to her and she was no longer the guide. At the brook she balked, so Tom sat down, took her head between his hands and looked into her eyes.

"We've got to make out without him, Una, each one of us, for a little while." He let the leash run its length through his fingers. She took a step or two, reached her nose into the water and drank, then she drew back and thrust herself against Tom's legs.

"You want to get on with it, don't you? All right, up the slope and to your new home. Hop up. That's a good girl."

She scarcely needed the urging once she had accepted the fact that she was to walk beside him. Up the hill they went, Tom's stride was still long and strong, but he took the climb slowly. Dropping his hand to rest on the domed head, feeling the big body against his legs, he was aware of the support she was giving him. And when he pushed the door of the house open, loneliness did not go in with him. He had someone to talk to again.

Before Una would eat the meal Tom had ready for her, she inspected the house, foot by foot, room by room, every corner, every piece of furniture. When she had satisfied herself about her surroundings, she returned to the kitchen and to the bowl of food. She ate slowly, licked the last crumb, took a long drink and joined Tom in the other room. She pushed her nose up under his arm to get his attention. Once assured, she found her own place, curled herself into a circle, wrapped her tail around till it touched the tip of her nose and sighed. Her eyes were open, and she kept them on Tom.

"I didn't choose you, Una, anymore than you chose me, but here we are for better or worse, and I think it's going to be better for both of us."

Knowing he was talking to her, she got up and crossed the intervening space to stand beside him. Tom reached into a pocket for the tag he had acquired earlier that day, the tag that had her name on it and his, with address and telephone number as well. He clamped it to the ring on her collar with her license and vaccination. She put her big paw on his knee, then he took her head between his hands and looked deep into her eyes.

"We're friends," Tom told her, sealing their relationship. He put his arms around her and hugged her to him. He could see the long black tail with its tan underside moving. "Good girl, such a good girl."

Una settled down near him and started to lick her paws, then her legs and wherever she could reach. She even went behind and around her ears like a cat. It was clear that she felt at home. Tom was relieved that the certainty of his love had gotten through to her. Always he had taken a dog's love for granted, but with this seventh one he could not only take, he must give in kind. That was a condition Gareth had laid upon him, not casually and not lightly.

Much later when he went upstairs to bed, Una followed him slowly, step by step. Nell used to fly up the stairs as if they weren't there. Una settled into the corner where Tom had put her blanket. Sometime, long after he had put out the light, he was aware that she was standing beside his bed, though he had not heard her get up or cross the room. Suppliant sounds were coming from deep within her, as if she couldn't get out what she wanted to say.

"I expect you're wondering where Gareth is," Tom said gently as he put his hand on her head, then ran it down her shoulder with a series of pats. After a while she left him and went, as silently as she had come, back to her blanket. He never heard a sound from her all night. Her breathing was quiet, and if she changed position, it was done without disturbance.

During their first weeks together, Tom was the learning one. Una was slow moving almost to the point of

being ponderous, especially in the house. It was as if
everything she did was done with respect to Tom. She
took steps cautiously, preceding him so she could com-
municate a change in a level or divert him from a piece
of furniture. Even their walks were plodding as she
fitted her gait to his. Off leash she would run, but in the
same careful way. Tom ached when he remembered
the way Nell had danced over the grass on fairy feet,
scarcely touching the ground, her plumy tail streaming
out in the wind of her running. He longed for her gaiety, her constant busyness, the demands she made on
him always in fun and for fun. He yearned for the way
she would leap against him when she wanted attention,
stand behind his chair and bark imperatively when she
thought he had sat long enough at his desk. Una was so
silent, so serious. Often she would stand before him
with a puzzled, worried look in her brown eyes. Perhaps in her way she was comparing him with Gareth
and was missing the need she had filled for her blind
master. Trained to a vocation, she was now without it.
Tom chided himself for making comparisons and tried
to assure Una by his words and frequent embraces that
in being company for him she was doing her work, a
work in any case.

Her first show of happiness was on the day he took
her to the Aurora. On leash and close at heel, he made
a round of calls with her, and she seemed to be in a new

element. She approached people in a courteous but reserved way as she responded to Tom's introductions to his acquaintances. When they reached Mrs. Sidway's room, she went through the formalities, then, at a command from Tom, lowered herself to the floor and made no further move.

After a half hour Mrs. Sidway exclaimed, "I've never seen such a well-behaved animal."

"It's her training. She knows I can see, but I want to keep her under command at times so she'll be ready to work with Gareth when he comes back."

Mrs. Sidway had developed an interest in the blind boy and always asked for the latest news. Tom gave her what there was, but it was scant, a postcard now and then but never in his own hand. He was in a good high school, and his marks were the best. He hoped to qualify for some kind of scholarship aid that would help him toward college.

"What draws him to the law?" Mrs. Sidway asked. "That will be another three years, even after the four of college?"

"For one thing, his father was a lawyer, so something having to do with jurisprudence may run in the family; for another, it's strictly practical. He feels that the law is a profession where his handicap will serve him."

"Be an asset, you mean. But how?"

"In that he won't be moved by appearances, only by

facts. Somewhere isn't justice represented by the figure of a woman, blindfolded, holding a pair of scales?"

"Mmm," Mrs. Sidway murmured. "Well, he's got a head for business as well as for legal matters."

Conscientious about Gareth's insistence on Una's need for exercise, Tom often found it trying. A walk to her was more a time for smelling than for gallivanting. It was all new territory, and exploring it was serious business to Una, tedious to Tom. She seemed to have to discover every inch of the way for herself, pushing her nose deep into the snow or against the earth. Tom presumed that she had to be sure she could find her way back to the house, not only for herself but for him. He felt impatient with her at times, but her slowness was not dawdling; it had a purpose. And he was ready to forgive her anything when she came back to him and nestled her nose in his hand. She would look up at him, asking with her eyes if there was not something she could do for him. He thanked her, fondled her, and she lapped his face in her appreciation. It was different from Nell's swift kisses, but it was her way.

And they were getting on to each other. Tones were understood, gestures interpreted. Still silent except for the deep sounds that came from far within her, it was up to Tom to decode the message. She had a way of talking in her sleep, murmurings that seemed to spell contentment. She had worn her responsibility like a garment during their first weeks; she began to shed it as they grew into each other's ways. Never in the house, but when they were outdoors, she had moments of playfulness.

Playing with a tennis ball, she proved to be a good catcher, returning it to Tom's hand so the game could go on. An old glove of his given to her proved to be something she could pounce on, then toss it in the air high above her head and leap to catch it as it came down. Once, in an especially lively mood, she went back on her haunches and waved her front paws playfully at Tom, curling her lips back in the equivalent of a smile.

"Whoever taught you to do that, or is it just something you picked up for yourself?"

She did it in moments of high pleasure, she did it in moments of urgency when, unless a door was opened quickly, there might be serious trouble, and she did it in contrition when Tom rebuked her for some misdemeanor. This happened rarely, but there was a time cookies disappeared from a plate when Tom had gone out to the kitchen to make tea. Not a crumb could be seen, but the plate was still in its place.

"Una!" Tom exclaimed, reproach in his tone.

Una went back on her haunches. She did not wave her paws but let them hang limply; her eyes were mournful; her nose quivered.

It was all Tom could do to get out the word *phooey*.

Una dropped to all fours, then reared up again in double apology. All Tom could do after that was love her. And she never again took food that was not hers, nor did Tom ever again leave a plate of goodies at nose level. Her supple tongue could be used for more than face washing.

He learned something about her philosophy one early spring day. The snow had gone, and the land was starting to dry up, so Tom went for a walk to the far field where Nell had had her digging project and had solved the mystery of Tagalong. Una ran ahead. She had, increasingly, been shedding her serious ways and a walk could now be a romp when once it had been a responsibility. She found a stick, tossed it into the air and caught it. She did it over and over, pleased with herself and well aware that Tom was watching her.

As they approached the old oak bole, Una dropped the stick and ran ahead to smell it carefully. When she came to the tumble of rocks where roots lay exposed and rotting, she sunk her nose down among them but was soon satisfied and moved along the bole in search of other smells. Tom drew near the rocks, thinking how far down now were the two who had locked themselves into a death struggle so many years ago. The earth was soft, and his left leg began sinking. Giving it a yank dislodged some of the stones, wedging his foot among them. Tom bent over to lift some away, and more slid in from the pile. He pulled again on his leg, but the more he pulled the more tightly wedged it became. He felt like an animal caught in a leg trap, and panic seized him. He was a long way from help, and even had he shouted, there was no one near enough to hear him.

Before he could call Una's name, she had come trotting back to stand beside him. Tilting her head first to one side, then the other, she knew he was in trouble and was ready for his command.

"You've got to do something, Una. It looks as if I'm here to stay." He pulled on his leg again, but, deep in the soft earth and covered by stones, it would not give.

Una put her paw on his right knee. The pressure, slight as it was, toppled Tom into a sitting position, right knee drawn up to his chest, left leg calf deep in the ground. Una sat down beside him.

"Go, Una," he gestured back over the way they had come. "Get help."

She looked at him, then lowered herself down beside him, placing her head on his left knee, never taking her eyes from his face.

Tom was annoyed. If it had been Victor, he could have said, "Go to Julie," and Victor would have been off across the field, searched out Julie and given her no peace until he had brought her to where Tom was.

"Go, Una, go, get help. I'm stuck." He pushed hard

against her. Panic turned to anger, and he flung his arm at her to send her off.

Una did not move, only pressed herself closer to him, only looked at him more intently.

Tom, overcome with remorse at his lack of control, put his arms around her, and something of her calm began to get through to him. He knew she would not leave him. The day might end, darkness and chill night might come and the long hours until morning, but she would give him the warmth of her body, the comfort of her presence. Tom held her head and looked into her eyes, nose touched nose, the warm tongue drew itself in an arc across his cheek.

"What went into a hole can come out of a hole," Tom said aloud to himself and to Una.

For a few moments he did nothing then, gradually from his sitting position, he moved the left foot tentatively, lifting a stone and then another from it. In time the foot came free. He pulled it out and stretched his leg, looking at it as if it were nice to make acquaintance with it again. Una left his side and stood over the released leg, pawing at it gently. Her eyes were on Tom.

"You knew it would come out if I took it easily, didn't you?" He reached his arms toward her, and she came into his embrace. "Good girl," he whispered, "good girl."

Later, when they walked back across the field, Tom limping from the stiffness in his ankle, Una walked close beside him, pressing her body against his left thigh in support.

Tom was always glad to be able to bring tidbits of news when he called at the Aurora, and this recent experience was worth relating. No chess game was in progress, so Ben and Mrs. Sidway gave him their entire attention. He enlarged on it, making his predicament worse and Una's refusal to do anything more annoying. And he had it all his own way because Una, after her usual polite greeting, had settled herself into sleep and could neither correct nor contest him.

"Imperturbable!" Tom exclaimed. "I couldn't get her to go for help. She insisted on sitting beside me, looking at me with those mournful eyes. I wanted to shake the daylights out of her, but I didn't have the strength. I wanted her to bark, to do something."

"And it never occurred to you that she had thought it all out and was doing the best possible thing under the circumstances?"

"What do you mean, Mrs. Sidway?"

"She was calming you down so you could free yourself, once you had stopped all your frantic pushing and pulling that only made matters worse."

"But why didn't she go for help? She's intelligent enough to know that people live only a mile or so away and that they could have come to me."

"Yes," Mrs. Sidway agreed, "and she might have figured out something else. She's a big dog, Tom, and not too well known in the neighborhood yet. Can you think what the reaction would have been if she had gone up to a man and grabbed at his trousers to get attention? It could have been misunderstood as an attack, and then you know what might have happened. You'd still be trapped. She did the only thing she could do—steady you so you would come to your senses."

Tom looked across the room at Una, flat out in sleep, her chest moving with the rhythm of her breathing, her tail quivering as if a dream were pleasant.

"You've got a lot to learn from that dog, Tom Wilson, and time is running out for you as it is for me. Now, tell me about the boy."

Tom related the latest news. Gareth's marks were high, and he would graduate in June with honors. He was doing construction work with Mr. Banneker on weekends and would continue during part of the summer.

"To earn money for college?"

Tom shook his head. "Just for his board."

"That boy should go to college."

"My thoughts exactly, and then on to law school."

"What's to keep him from doing what his heart is set on?"

Tom stared. Had she never heard of the cost of such

an education. What a question! "I'll help all I can, and
he should be in line for some scholarship aid."

"And the people he's been placed with. Won't they
give some help?"

Tom shook his head. "Manual work is all they can see
for him."

"Well, he's got brains as well as hands. What's more,
he knows what he wants to do with his life. What did
you say his name was?"

"Gareth Granger."

Mrs. Sidway repeated it without comment.

Una stood up and shook herself, then she crossed the
room to Tom and thrust her head under his arm. He
knew her signal.

"We'll come again in a few days," Tom said.

"Thanks," she took his outstretched hand in hers,
"you always give me something to look forward to, and
that," she said with an emphasis new to her, "is life."

Warm days in April took the last vestiges of snow
away, and ice had gone from the lakes. Tom had a
longing for the water and was eager to see if Una would
take to the canoe as other dogs had. If not, she would
be willing to wait on the shore. His pack and jacket laid
at the foot of a tree would be base enough for her and
assurance of his return. The longer she was with him,
the more he realized that all she wanted was to be
where he was, doing what he did, going where he went,

and waiting for him outside or in the car if it was a place
where dogs did not go.

Stately when walking beside him on a street or in the
town, Una was different on the road to the lake. Once
they had left the car and started off, Una sensed adventure. She raced ahead, then raced back to him as he
came more slowly down the wood road. She leaped
over a fallen tree and scrambled up a boulder to stand
on its top and survey her surroundings. She gave chase
to a squirrel, but wisely avoided a slow-moving porcu-
pine, then she soon returned to Tom.

"It's a good world, isn't it, Una," he said, fondling her,
"and a good day for what we want to do; and you're a
good dog."

Running on ahead of him, Una reached the lake first.
She halted, then approached cautiously. Discovering
what it was, she had a long drink, waded in, swam a few
yards, then turned and swam back again. Standing on
the shore, she shook herself vigorously and waited for
Tom. When he reached her she sat back on her haunches and waved her paws excitedly, the singing sound
came from deep within her, even her lips curled back
in a smile. That she approved was evident. Tom took off
his jacket, laid it and his pack near a tree, then brought
the canoe and paddle out from the shelter. Sliding the
canoe into the water and taking his place, he called to
Una to come with him; but this she did not approve.

With all the precision of which she was capable, she made her preference clear. She would wait on the shore for his return.

"See you when I get back," he called as he pushed the canoe off and on its way.

She looked completely agreeable. The "see you" was a sound she understood. It meant only one thing, and that was that he would come back; *when* had no bearing on the fact.

The sun was high, the water calm, its surface disturbed only by the ripples made by the passage of the canoe. Tom paddled slowly, searching for signs of spring along the shore. It was too early for many of them, but there was a feeling in the air that doors were opening, doors that had been locked by cold and ice and snow all during the winter. If he could find mayflowers, he would know for sure that spring was at hand. He headed the canoe into a cove, got out and pulled it half out of the water. He looped its rope to a birch tree, laid the paddle flat on the bottom, and went to the place where he and Julie had first found mayflowers and sought them every spring thereafter.

A few yards from shore, where snow had retreated early, there they were with their often misshapen leaves and wirey stems. Most of them were still tightly budded, but a few were open, and their fragrance was unmistakable. Tom knelt more in reverence than to

gather a few, cutting the stems carefully and rolling
them in moss to keep their freshness, then he tucked
the little bunch into the breast pocket of his shirt. So
great was his joy, and such a flood of memories were
brought to him by these first flowers of the year, that he
sat down near them. The sun was becoming veiled, and
the day was losing warmth, but he decided to rest for
a little while in what had become through the years a
hallowed secret spot. Stretching out on the ground, his
fingers played among the flowers while he breathed
their sweetness. Closing his eyes, he gave himself to the
sleep that came often and easily these days, and at
unexpected moments. "Fifteen minutes," he told himself, "then I'll go back to Una."

When he awoke, he had no idea of the time. He was
cold and stiff from lying on the ground and was en-
veloped in mist. He sat up and shook his arms, then one
leg after the other to get circulation going. It might
have been evening, for the mist had grayed everything
so completely. He could see nothing beyond the tip of
his outstretched booted feet, but he could hear water
lapping on the shore. The sound was his guide, and with
it he crawled to the canoe. Finding the birch first, he
put his hands around it and let it help him to stand;
feeling for the rope, he undid it, then placed his hands
on the bow of the canoe, reached for the paddle and
soon pushed himself away from the shore. But how was

he to get his direction? He would make little headway if he followed the shore line, for there were too many submerged rocks for good paddling.

He thrust off into the lake and turned the way he had come, trusting to an inner compass. The mist rolled over him in deepening waves. He thought of Una sitting near his gear, waiting silently for him. Paddling hard helped ward off some of the dampness from the air. He was confident in his sense of direction and expected any moment to see the familiar little beach with Una sitting there, her head up and ears pointed; he strained his ears for the rumble of sound he knew she would make in her relief at his return. But all he saw after long paddling was the white birch to which he had tied the canoe at what now seemed an age ago.

He slapped hard at the water in his annoyance and again as he pushed out from the shore. He turned the bow in a different direction and hallooed into the mist. The echo of his own voice came back to him, muffled and almost unrecognizable. Placing the paddle carefully down, he cupped his hands to his mouth to increase the sound.

"Una!" he called into the air, the mist, the nothingness. "Una!" then he waited.

From what seemed half a world away came an answering bark. Tom listened, but it did not come again. Tom picked up his paddle and tried to hold himself in the direction from which the sound had come.

"Una!"

Once again came the bark, a little nearer this time, a little clearer.

So that was it. She would answer only in answer to his call. Deep-throated and muffled by the mist as it was, it could only be Una. There was no habitation with a likely dog within miles of the lake. By the third time he heard it, he knew for certain that it was Una, the silent one who had never barked before to his hearing. Sometimes the sound seemed to be more from the left, sometimes more from the right, but each time he corrected his direction to keep on course. She was doing for him with her voice what he had seen her do for Gareth with her eyes, guiding. He called, she answered, and he paddled toward the sound. He was in her care now, and he was willing to trust her concern.

He called. Now the answer was nearer, and he hastened toward it, though the tip of the bow was the limit of his vision.

"Una!"

The answer was so near that he slowed his stroke to avoid coming too hard against the shore.

"Una!"

There was a splash that rocked the canoe, and there she was, lifting her big head up to rest it on the gunnel, looking at him with eyes as dark as the water. He rode the canoe up onto the little beach near where his gear was lying at the base of a tree. Wet and dripping, she nuzzled him, pushing herself against him, impatient to have his face come to her level so she could lap it.

He had no words to say but her name and "Good dog, Una, such a good dog." He said it over and over again. The crooning sound she made told him she understood. Tom sank down on the ground near the tree, desperately tired from the exertion of paddling and the strain of being lost.

"You'll have to get us out of the woods, Una," he said. "I can't see any more among the trees than I could in the water with all this mist, but I've got to rest first."

She had to rest too and sat down beside him, stretching her full length along his length and providing warmth. Tom breathed deeply. The damp air was invigorating, the silence, the comfort Una gave, brought him to himself, and tiredness began to ease away. Soon he reached into his pack for the thermos of tea and the thick sandwich he had made. He put his hand on the biscuit he had brought for Una. She took it delicately, as she was accustomed to doing, more with her lips than her teeth. She held it between her paws and crunched it slowly, morsel by delectable morsel, while Tom had his meal.

Refreshed and rested, Tom put the canoe away, slung his pack over his shoulder and called to Una. She came to position at his left side as she had been trained to do by her blind master, eyes looking at him, ready for his command. He laid his hand on her back, then worked his fingers up to her collar. "Forward," he said, hoping the duty she had to carry through for him would be as evident to her as when she wore her harness and responded to Gareth.

She started slowly, deliberation in every step. Preceding him by a few inches, she changed her pace at any unevenness in the terrain so that he could adjust himself to it. When she seemed to veer from a straight line, he saw that a rock had loomed in their path. He had not the slightest idea where she was leading him, but he trusted her implicitly. He said her name often to keep contact, and he followed it with the words that were her music, "Good girl, such a good girl." As the wood road rose, Tom began to make out the shapes of trees among which they were moving. He could even see the road itself for a few feet ahead of them. It was the one they had gone over with such abandon earlier in the day.

Suddenly, as if gray curtains had been drawn aside, they were out of the mist and into pale sunshine. The first warmth of the year meeting the still-frigid water of the lake had caused the mist, and it existed only near the water. The day was far from bright, but it was not even late afternoon, and evening was still far off. When they reached the car, Una came to a full stop. She sat back on her haunches and looked at Tom. This was where he had wanted to go.

Tom leaned against the car. Often, coming up the old

road with its sharp rise and uneven ground, he had become out of breath and needed to rest to regain strength and wind, but this time it had been so gradual, so slow, and the support of the big body against his thigh had been so comforting that he was breathing as naturally as if they had been walking on the level. He returned Una's gaze and told her what a good girl she was, then he told her how much he loved her. His heart was in his words, and she knew it. She put her front paws against his chest and lapped his face.

On the drive home, Tom thought of the story he would have to tell Mrs. Sidway. He even had three budded mayflowers in his pocket to give her. They might remind her of springs she had known. She had been recalling more of the good things of her life of late, and the flowers, tiny and few as they were, might bring back some memory of days when she too had sought them.

But it was too late when he got home to visit the Aurora, and he was ready for some warm food, then a hot bath and bed. Another day would come soon enough, and the flowers would keep. He put them in water, and soon their fragrance made itself known in the room. Una ate her supper with relish. Soon after, she went to the corner where her blanket was and curled herself up into sleep. It had been a day for her, too.

Demands on Tom's time and work to be done kept

him from his usual visit to the Aurora for several days. When he had a free afternoon, the flowers were no longer fresh, but they were fresh in his mind, and Tom decided that to tell Mrs Sidway about them and about how he had fallen asleep among them, then wakened to find the world lost in mist, might mean more to her than placing the few flowers in her hands. Most of all, he wanted to tell her about Una, the silent one, and what she had done.

Ben looked at him strangely when Tom stopped in at his room. "You haven't heard, then?"

"What?"

"Mrs. Sidway died last night. There's someone else in her room now."

"What about her family? Has anyone come?"

Ben shook his head. "There was no one left. That's why, or one reason anyway, that she was so lonely."

Tom told Ben the story of the day on the lake, then he stayed long enough to play a game of checkers. When he called to Una and started down the hall toward the front door, Una preceded him. She was accustomed to turning in at Mrs. Sidway's room ahead of him, but this time she did not so much as cast a glance at the open door. Straight to the front door she went, then sat down until Tom would come to open it.

A nurse came out of the office. She smiled a greeting. "Ben told you about Mrs. Sidway?"

Tom nodded.

"This happens often here, but sometimes the letting go of life is not easy even for those for whom it no longer has any meaning. With Mrs. Sidway it was so simple, just breathing that grew shorter and fainter. She kept saying, 'It's all right now, it's all right now.' "

"Had she had any visitors?"

"No one but her attorney. He used to come every month, but lately he's been coming every week. It seems she had a lot of papers to sign."

"Thanks for telling me." Tom repeated the words, " 'It's all right now.' " He turned away. The nurse's eyes were moist.

"For the past two years or so, ago, she had become so difficult, none of us thought she would meet the end easily, but she did. Used as we are to it, it helps us all when it's taken serenely."

"You must have done a lot for her."

"We did what we could, but it was your little dog who gave her what she needed. It opened her up, made her think of others."

"Thanks," Tom said again, and quickly, for now he could not get to the door soon enough.

Una was waiting. He slipped two fingers from his left hand around her collar and opened the door with his right. Again he was walking in a mist, but this time it was of his own making.

"Una, forward, and home," he said. His voice was

little more than a whisper but quite loud enough for one whose pointed ears were ready for a summons to work.

She led him slowly, pausing at curbs, turning corners cautiously, crossing streets as if she was the one who commanded the flow of traffic. Long before they reached home, Tom's eyes had cleared, and he could see quite well for himself, but he had given Una a charge, and until their destination was reached, he could not release her from it.

A week later Tom had a telephone call from a man who identified himself as David Martin of the firm of Martin and Ormsby, Attorneys-at-Law. He asked to see Tom and indicated that the matter was important and confidential. They set a day, and Tom filled the time between wondering how it was that a lawyer wanted to see him. He could not recall having run afoul of the law —breaking the speed limit, fishing out of season; and he was reasonably sure that Una was no culprit. Always near him, she could not have caused trouble with a neighbor's flock of sheep nor even a cat. Perhaps someone wanted to buy his land, and this might be the first move.

It was land that had been in the family since the first Wilson had settled there and worked it more than a hundred years ago, and the nursery part of it was still productive. It had lost value as farmland, and many of the fields were being taken over by nature, going back to brush and some to woodland, for Tom followed a tree-planting sequence through the years. It was land that had appreciated in value as real estate, since it was close enough to the town to offer choice building sites. Tom had no intention of selling any of it until he knew clearly what Gareth's needs might be. If his intentions really were for college, the land might be the means of helping him get through college and into law school. Wondering, speculating, he waited for Mr. Martin's visit.

Una's ears pricked at the sound of a car stopping, then at footsteps coming up the walk. She made no move until the bell rang, then she accompanied Tom to the door and stood beside him while he opened it. Together they greeted Mr. Martin, briefcase in hand.

"But I thought you had a little dog, one of those small collies?" Mr. Martin said as Una nudged him politely, wagging her tail; then she withdrew a few paces and sat down to observe the situation.

"Yes, I did, up until a few months ago. This is Una. She doesn't really belong to me. I'm just giving her a home."

They went in to the sitting room, and Tom gestured to a chair. Mr. Martin sat down and opened his briefcase, bringing out a sheaf of papers.

"You are, I believe, related to a young man by the name of Gareth Granger."

Tom shook his head. "Not related formally, but in a friendly way. Una is his dog, his guide dog."

Mr. Martin consulted his papers. "Yes, my client understood that Mr. Granger was without sight. And without means."

"Your client?"

"Mrs. Edwina Sibbons Sidway, who died on April 24th at the age of ninety. This is her last will and testament. In it you are mentioned as guardian of Gareth Granger. Your address was given, but none for Mr. Granger. Tell me, Mr. Wilson, what you know about him."

Una had risen and crossed the room in her deliberate way. She stood beside Mr. Martin, then laid her head on his knee, resting it there.

"Do you mind her?" Tom asked.

"Not at all. In fact I feel rather flattered by her attention."

"She's smart enough to know that what affects Gareth Granger is going to affect her, and I guess she wants to be in on it."

"To protect his interests?"

"Could be."

Tom told Gareth's story, as much as he knew of it— the accident occurring when he was six that had blinded him and taken the lives of his parents. He had become the charge for four years each of three separate families. He was still under the care of the Bannekers and would be until he was eighteen. He had attended a school for the blind and gained skills needed to get on with his life. Fairly recently he had obtained a dog, who meant much to him but was apparently too much for the Bannekers, who made their home in a trailer. Mr. Banneker followed construction jobs around the country.

"When I met Gareth in the woods, he had been given three days to dispose of the dog because the Bannekers were moving to the Southwest."

"He was not totally dependent on the dog, then?"

"No, he had been taught other ways of getting around, along with braille and much else. I saw him just once with a special long cane. He handled himself with grace, and that was in the woods."

"What is ahead for Mr. Granger?"

"As much as I know—and this is from one conversation with Mr. Banneker and two letters during the past six months—he graduates from high school in Phoenix, Arizona, in June; but he will not be eighteen until the first of August. At that time Gareth becomes his own man, but between June and August Mr. Banneker wants him to work for him to pay for some of his board."

"And Mr. Granger?" Mr. Martin was stroking Una's head as he asked questions.

"He wants to go on to college. Law school is his hope and impossible dream."

"There is no money, then?" Tom felt there was so much he did not know that any answer he gave could only be problematical. "I think what the boy's father had was distributed to the families who cared for Gareth, brought him up."

Una raised her head from its rest on Mr. Martin's knee and went to sit near Tom, easing her body down and putting her head on her front legs; eyes were open, ears were pricked, but she was relaxed.

Mr. Martin had been making notes, and almost to himself he said, "It may not be an impossible dream. I'll need the address of Mr. Banneker because this will have to be checked into very carefully."

"What exactly?" Tom asked, curious but unwilling to push for information until Mr. Martin was ready to give it.

"For years, Mr. Wilson, my firm has managed the Sidway estate, and it is considerable. When Mr. Sidway died ten years ago, everything was left to Mrs. Sidway. They both outlived their only child, who never married, so there were no dependents. Mrs. Sidway has refused to make a will, even though I have called on her with this express purpose, every month since she went to the Aurora Nursing Home. Her mind was perfectly clear, but her heart was—shall we say—warped? A series of unhappy events in her life seemed to turn her into herself. She made things difficult for everyone at the home, often refusing to speak to anyone and then only abruptly. I told her what would happen to her estate if she left no will, but that seemed to have no effect on her. Her feeling was that life had been unkind to her, so why should she show any kindness. Then she began to change. She started telling me about a little dog who came and sat with her for an hour or so quite often. Without words they understood each other. Much as I enjoy dogs, Mr. Wilson, it didn't make sense to me, and from her description it was not this dog."

"No, it was not Una."

"About a month ago she sent for me and told me she was ready to make a will. You were mentioned as guardian of the young man, address not known, named Gareth Granger. She had thought it all out very carefully—I'll leave the copy with you for you to study—a sufficient sum of money is to be paid every year to the college Mr. Granger attends; this is to continue through his years of law school, then it will cease. Whatever remains, and even that, I dare say, will be considerable, is to be used as an endowment for the college and law school attended." Mr. Martin shook his head. "I've drawn up many wills, Mr. Wilson, but this was one of the most unusual and one that holds ongoing helpfulness." He handed Tom the copy.

Tom's eyes rested on the opening words, "I, Edwina Sibbons Sidway, being of sound mind but frail in body, do by this instrument . . ." Tom found it hard to read further.

Mr. Martin said, "I'm leaving that copy with you, but I shall need your signature on some papers. Will you come to my office at your earliest convenience? This does not go into effect, of course, until Mr. Granger reaches the age of eighteen and returns to make his home with you. You will be, to all intents and purposes, his next of kin."

"It's like a fairy tale," Tom said, trying to shake himself into the grasp of the situation.

"Good things do happen," Mr. Martin said as he gathered up his papers and put them back into his briefcase, "but sometimes we have to wait, and sometimes they hang on the thinnest threads of circumstance. Now, if I may have Mr. Banneker's address."

After the attorney left, Tom went out to the garden and sat on the bench where he had sat so often with Julie, where she had sat so often with Victor on one side, and where he had sat alone. Una followed him and settled herself close enough for him to reach out to her if he so wanted. Spring was in the garden in the thrust of bulbs and the swelling of buds; spring was in Tom's heart.

Soon Una moved closer to Tom to rest her head on his knees, then she went back on her haunches and waved her paws gaily at him.

"You want a walk? Well, so do I." And together they were off.

Una raced ahead, Tom came more slowly, over the brook and up to the hemlock stand. At the flat stone where he had first met her with Gareth, he thought she might sniff around it, but she paid no attention to it. Tom watched her as she gave herself to the moment, tracking a scent, snuffling around a tree; he realized that more and more he was learning to do just that, not looking back with longing or ahead with uncertainty but taking the present for what it was.

Following her lead deeper into the woods on a trail that was littered with the debris of winter, he picked up branches as he went along, feeling satisfaction in the tidying. Una never went beyond the range of his sight, and he knew she kept herself within call. Weariness caught up with Tom, and he stopped his trail clearing. Once he could go all day without protest from his body; now he had to recognize its signals. The years had weight even when inwardly he felt no different from the boy who had romped with Bre'er.

Leaning against one of the big hemlocks, he looked up into its maze of branches. New green tips were showing, and he thought of the century or more the tree had been growing, withstanding storms, taking heat and cold, wind, rain, ice and snow. They were all part of its life and had gone to make it what it was. He breathed deeply in a rhythm he had found restorative, and gradually the tiredness ebbed away, and something of the tree became his.

He took from his pocket the wooden whistle Gareth had made and given him and blew on it. Una heard and made an arabesque in midair to face the direction from which the sound had come. She saw him leaning against the tree and in a few swift leaps came to stand before him. Her stance, the searching look in her eyes, the slight quivering in the muscles of her forelegs all were saying, "What can I do for you?"

Tom put two fingers under her collar, and she swerved her body to his left side, pressing it against his thigh. "Without you, Una, I'd find the way back a bit tiring," he fondled her ears playfully, "but without you I wouldn't have come to the woods. Forward."

Una walked sedately, carefully, suiting her pace to Tom's as they went through the woods, stopped by the brook for a drink, then up the slope. Tom looked at the house as they approached. It had seen much living, much loving, now it would be home for Gareth of the large hands and Una of the strong body.

During the weeks that followed there were many visits to the office of Martin and Ormsby, many letters written, many documents signed. When it was all completed, it came down to two very simple facts: Gareth would make his home with Tom from the time he was eighteen, and he would receive once a year from the firm of Martin and Ormsby the amount needed for his education: four years of college, three of law school, then it would terminate and go to others. Tom would be responsible for board; any extra Gareth would earn himself. Mrs. Sidway had been strict with herself, reason enough for the money to accumulate as it had in the estate; she would be strict with others.

"You must feel good at the way it's all working out," Ben said one summer day as they sat in the garden at the Aurora. Una lying close by was restful but alert to all that was going on around her.

"Oh, I do," Tom agreed, "and by the thinnest threads of circumstance."

"What's that?"

"A phrase the lawyer used."

That night after Tom had gone to bed and Una was sleeping on her blanket in her corner of the room, Tom put out the light and expected sleep to come reasonably soon. He was tired enough, but sleep was not always the sequence. Eyes closed, but wide awake, he was caught up in memory. He thought of Julie, of the years they had had and of the longing he felt to share life with her again. He heard no sound, no padded footsteps, but he was aware of a big head resting itself on the edge of the bed, of a warm breath blowing toward him. He turned his head. There was just enough light from a waning moon for him to see Una's eyes looking at him, just looking; so he looked back. He was not near enough to receive a caress from her tongue, nor would she have given it. If he chose to ignore her, she would return to her corner as silently as she had come from it.

Tom kept looking into her eyes, knowing that she had sensed his heartache and had come to give him the only comfort she could—her presence. After a while he brought out his hand from under the sheet and laid it on her head. When he withdrew it, she turned and went back to her corner, settling herself with a sigh that Tom interpreted as satisfaction. The next thing he knew, light was flooding the room, and it was morning.

As the weeks went by, Una seemed to grow increasingly attentive. Her whole interest was to be with Tom, and she followed him or sought him out. There were many words she knew well and reacted to, but with long sentences she cocked her ears, twisting her head first to one side then the other, searched Tom with her eyes in the endeavor to determine all that he was saying. Often, in mockery at the tediousness of words, she would sit back on her haunches, tongue lolling from open mouth in a sort of canine laughter, and her eyes searching him in a "Let's do something" way. Tom would respond with a show of affection, a game with a ball or an old glove, even a dance of delight on the lawn.

He had never had such attention from a dog, even

though he could look back over a life that had scarcely ever been without a dog; but it worried him. Una was not his dog, she was Gareth's. It was Gareth who needed her and would in the years ahead far more than he might now. Would she leave his side and go to Gareth's? He talked to her about Gareth, and she tilted her head from one side to the other. He even tried to get her to lead him when they went walking, closing his eyes, bumping and stumbling along. She took it as a game, and Tom remembered that without her harness she was any dog, only with it was she a guide dog. He moved her blanket into the room on the ground floor that would be Gareth's to get her used to sleeping there, but when his back was turned, she took it in her teeth and dragged it up the stairs to the room she shared with Tom.

"You're Gareth's dog, Una, not mine," he said to her firmly.

She looked at him, eyes unblinking.

The time came when she would be put to the test.

It was a warm day early in August. According to the last letter received from Gareth he would come on the two-thirty bus. One suitcase was all he had; a box with his braille books was being mailed. He had not collected much during the months he had been living in the trailer, for space was so limited.

Tom got to the bus station half an hour early in case the bus was ahead of time. Instead it came in half an hour late. Sitting in the waiting room with Una beside him, Tom tried to calm his excitement, tried not to think of tomorrow and tomorrow, of next year and the next. He felt Una become alert. Tom saw the bus turn slowly down the street and into the station yard. Una placed front paws on his knees and made the thrumming sound, almost a moaning, indicative of emotion that must find its way out in some form. Tom put his hand on her head. "Una, rest." She sat down at the command, but every muscle was quivering.

The bus rolled to a stop. The door was opened, and people started emerging. Gareth was the last. Standing in the open doorway, his long cane swung sideways to get the width, then dropping down to get the depth of the first step, then the second, then to the pavement. In his other hand he carried his one piece of baggage, and to it was strapped Una's harness. In the brief time that it took Gareth to come down the three steps, Tom saw that he had grown taller; tanned from the sun in the Southwest, his hair had lightened to a wheat color. He stood erect; he looked self-confident.

Una was straining at the hold Tom had on her collar and making guttural sounds. Tom had no need to say any word. She knew where they were going and to whom. Tom loosed the hold he had on her so that she could be the first to greet Gareth. Leaping, she soared through the intervening space but did not hurl herself against Gareth. She drew herself and all her quivering emotion together and came to a halt, sitting down in front of him and pushing her head between his knees. Gareth set the suitcase down and dropped to his knees beside her. His arms went around her, feeling their way across her shoulders, then along her thick coat to the tail that was moving rapidly. He whispered into her ear. She lapped his face. Tom heard the traditional words, "Good dog, Una, such a good dog."

Gareth stood up and held out his hand. While Tom grasped it, Una nuzzled the harness strapped to the suitcase.

"You've come home."

"Yes."

One word held the future in it.

They did not talk much until they reached the Wilson house and sat down on the porch. Una, worn out by emotion, lay between them and soon lost herself in sleep. There was much to say, and yet there was a feeling that most of it could wait. The journey had been long, two nights and a day on the bus, and Gareth was soon ready to go to bed. When Tom took him into the room that would be his, Una followed. In a corner near the bed Tom had placed her blanket. There was no question now but that here it would stay.

Tom started to explain the layout of the room, but Gareth interrupted, "Una will show me. It won't be the first time we've made our own inspection."

"Shall I give you a call in the morning?"

"If you like, but Una has a good time sense. She'll get me up as soon as she hears you stirring."

"It won't be early, Gareth, you've got some sleeping to do to make up for all that traveling."

Gareth's smile was one of total agreement. "Una's in great condition, Tom. Thanks for keeping her, for taking such good care of her."

"She took pretty good care of me."

"I knew she would."

"Shall I put out the light?"

"If anyone's going to, you'd better. That's one thing Una's never learned to do."

Tom chided himself for not remembering.

Later, but not much later, when Tom went upstairs to his room, he had the good feeling that there was another person in the house. There had been a presence in Una for the past many months, but this time it was a human being. Even though Gareth would be going off to college, he would still be here in his clothes and his books and his belongings, and he would be coming back for vacations during the year. There would be the summer months to look forward to. There was much to think and talk about together, there were many decisions to be made and questions to be answered, but Tom stilled his mind and held to the one thing he knew: Gareth was here, a part of his life, and Una was a part of both their lives.

It was the small whiffling sound, the warm breath across his face that woke Tom, not the daylight in his room. Opening his eyes, he turned his head slightly to look at Una, resting her head on the edge of his bed and gazing at him. Eyes met eyes, and for a space of time everything that needed to be said was said. Tom placed his hand on her head. She made her deep crooning sound, low, quiet, only for him, then she backed slowly away, her eyes on him until she turned and went down the stairs to Gareth's room. He heard the careful steps, he heard the slight movement of the door as she pushed it open. He knew he would hear no more until he dressed and went down to the kitchen to get breakfast for them all. He had his answer to the question that had worried him. Una would be able to handle them both.

The next afternoon, sitting on the porch, they started on the long conversations that were necessary to fill in the gaps of their relationship and to plan for the years ahead. Gareth reached his hand down to rest it on Una. Not finding her in her usual place beside him, he called her name. There was no immediate response.

"I expect she felt she should give us a little time to ourselves," Gareth said. "She'll soon be back."

When Una came back, it was not in answer to whistle

or call but in custody of a very angry man. A piece of rope had been tied to her collar, and she was walking beside the man with measured pace and dignity unruffled. Behind trailed another dog, yellowish brown in color and of uncertain breed.

"Hello there, Ralston," Tom said, recognizing a farmer who lived down the road, "what brings you here?"

"Killed one of my lambs, your dog did, Tom Wilson. I knew she was yours, for I've seen you go by with her sitting in your car. I could put the law on you if you don't settle with me now and give me what that lamb was worth."

Tom introduced Gareth and asked Ralston to sit down. He suggested that Una be let loose from the rope.

"No, I will not. I don't want her to attack my dog."

"Una, sit," Gareth said in a low voice.

Una sat where she was, beside Ralston who had taken the chair Tom gestured to. The other dog hung back uncertainly.

Tom said, "Isn't that a new dog you have, Ralston?"

"Had him a few days. He's a mix. Plan to make a herder out of him. Guess he'll be a protection if a dog like yours is allowed to roam the countryside. Shouldn't be allowed to live, a dog that goes around killing other people's animals."

Then Gareth took over. Turning to face the farmer,

he asked, in a voice only a little louder than he had used to Una, "Please tell us the story as you witnessed it, Mr. Ralston. It happens that the Shepherd in question is mine, and I am the responsible one."

Gareth's glance never left Mr. Ralston as the story of the fracas was told. Tom watched intently, aware that he was seeing a future lawyer in action. Gareth listened. His hands lay open in his lap; at times he raised them slightly as if they were scales and in them the facts were being weighed. When the story was concluded, Gareth asked several questions.

"And you did not actually see this?"

"Not with my eyes. I heard the noise, and when I got there your dog was on top of mine, trying to kill him the way she had the lamb."

"Is there much blood on the Shepherd?"

Mr. Ralston seemed surprised at the question and looked down at Una. "No, not now, that is."

"And on your dog?"

"Some, but the mix was fighting to save his life from that killer of yours."

"Please refer to her as a Shepherd, Mr. Ralston, as you would in a court of law."

Gareth asked more questions, pausing after each answer as if noting it for further reference.

"Where is the lamb now?"

"In my freezer. Meat's too expensive these days to waste any."

"Mr. Ralston, you say you have not had your dog long enough for full training as a herder?"

"That's right. Got the mix just about a week ago."

"Is it possible that the mix might have attacked the lamb and that the Shepherd got herself involved endeavoring to save the lamb?"

"Not a chance. That big hound—Shepherd—has all the marks of a killer."

"Guilt must be proven, Mr. Ralston."

"Once it is, will you agree to have the Shepherd put out of the way?"

"I repeat that guilt must be proven."

"How you going to do that?"

"By the simple process of a gastric lavage."

"What's that?"

Gareth turned toward Tom. "Tom, be so good as to phone your veterinarian's office. Tell him the story and see when he can perform a lavage. Tell him we're in doubt about the contents of the stomachs of two dogs."

Tom went into the house to make the call.

Mr. Ralston shifted in his chair. He looked down at Una, then looked quickly away. "Don't you let that Shepherd take you in with those great big eyes of hers."

"That," Gareth smiled for the first time during the conversation, "is something that will not happen."

Tom was soon back. "We're in luck. Dr. Johns has just got in from making some calls. He says the sooner a lavage is done the better and that he can do it now."

"Who decides this case?" The farmer asked as he tossed the rope he was still holding to Tom.

"The evidence," Gareth said.

Tom untied the rope from Una's collar and slipped his fingers under it as he had so often. He gave the command "Forward," and they walked toward his car. Mr. Ralston took the rope in his hands and tied it around the collar of his dog. He followed Tom.

Gareth sat quietly while they were gone.

An hour later Tom came back with Una trotting beside him. At sight of Gareth she leaped up the steps of the porch and nuzzled against him. Gareth fondled her.

"Well?" Gareth asked.

"Well indeed. The mix's stomach was full of wool and other incriminating evidence. Una's had nothing but a few yellow hairs, which showed she had gone to the lamb's defense."

Gareth smiled and put his arms around Una. "Good girl, but don't take yourself off on walks again all by yourself. It isn't worth it."

She pushed her head under his armpit as the quickest way to get to his face and lap it, then she put one of her big paws on his knee and made her crooning sound.

"Where's the mix now?"

"Left with Dr. Johns to be despatched to whatever purgatory is reserved for canine malefactors. Ralston says he's going to get a dog like Una."

"A dog like Una!" Gareth exclaimed with feeling. "He can get a dog, but it will be up to him to make it a companion dog."

"That's what I told him."

"And where is Mr. Ralston?"

"Gone back to his freezer to cut a leg of frozen lamb for us to have."

"Oh, no!" Gareth laughed.

"He says it's the only way he knows how to repay you. He also said that if he'd known you were blind, he wouldn't have been so hard on you."

Gareth shook his head slowly. "He'll have to learn that blindness makes no difference. In my profession it can even be an asset."

Tom stared. Where had he heard that word used in almost the same way?

That night Tom had a rare dream: one that he recalled in all its clarity on waking and one whose interpretation gave him comfort.

He was in a great Gothic hall of a college, attending the awarding of degrees. It was a class of graduate students, and they were being given the degrees that would take them into their chosen professions. Each one, from the moment of stepping down from the platform, diploma in hand, would have as title after his name J.D., Judicial Doctor. Tom watched the antique formality as each one stepped forward and a handclasp was given, a presentation made. Moving away from the platform, each one walked down the aisle lined with people applauding, smiling.

One of the graduates walked forward to receive his degree, and beside him walked a dog. Presentation was made to the man, then another to the dog as a smaller diploma was placed carefully between its teeth. The people watching the procedure did more than smile and applaud; they rose and cheered. The hall echoed with their acclamation, not for the man or for the dog but for the team they made as they came down the steps and along the aisle. Tom's eyes misted at the sight, but they cleared enough for recognition when the two approached where he was standing: the dog was Nell, and the man whose fingers touched her collar was himself. He looked at Thomas Wilson, mortarboard on his white head, a broad smile on his lined face. Strange and wonderful it was to be both actor and observer; equally wonderful but not at all strange was the appearance of the two together.

Sometime he would tell Gareth about the dream, knowing that one who saw by insight rather than by sight would understand.